Concealing Fire

A Fiery Fairy Tale Novella

Dallas Fire & Rescue

(Kindle Worlds)

Bestselling Author

Siera London

Concealing Fire

Copyright © 2016 Katrina Pringle

Cover art by Fantasia Frog

Edited by Rebecca Martin of Bare Essentials Publishing
Edited by Gayla Leath of Dark Dreams Editing

This book is a work of fiction. Certain real locations are mentioned, however names, characters, events and incidents described in this book are a product of the author's imagination or used fictitiously. Any resemblance to actual events, real persons, living or deceased, is coincidental.

About This Book

Dallas Fire & Rescue firefighter, Kendall Raine goes out of her way to avoid male attention. She's focused on salvaging her career, and the temporary assignment to Key West's Historic District Firehouse is just the opportunity she's been waiting for. Unfortunately for Kendall, her hot as sin teammate threatens her focus and stokes an internal fire she thought long extinguished.

Firefighter and former Marine, Cutler Stevens sees beyond Kendall's disguise the moment he lays eyes on her. As a former Marine, his fighting days are behind him, but gut instinct tells him this woman could use a champion on her side. Cutler likes his life easy and his women uncomplicated, but attraction and curiosity spark a deep desire to uncover what Kendall is desperately trying to hide.

After a natural disaster forces them together, they surrender to the burning passion between them. Cutler knows one night with Kendall in his arms will never be enough, even if she won't admit it.

Just when Kendall accepts Cutler as a permanent part of her life, they are both tested when her past follows her to the southernmost point of the United States. How far will Cutler go when he discovers what Kendall is prepared to do to preserve her newfound freedom? Will their decisions protect their newfound love or unveil a secret that will consume them both?

Acknowledgements

Special thanks to Paige Tyler for creating the *Dallas Fire & Rescue* world filled with kick-butt heroines and sexy firefighters. I had a lot of fun letting my imagination run wild with this adaption of the Brothers Grimm's Little Red Riding Hood tale.

—To Fire Captain D. Austin, your input has been invaluable.

—To DesaRae and Courtney, thanks, ladies, for helping me assemble my research team.

—To Kate and Lanie, I thank you for sharing the scoop on what it's like to be a firefighter's lady.

—As always, to Mr. Awesome, Michele, Rebecca, Devri, and Gayla you are my sounding board, my support network, my critique partner, my editor; in other words, you are amazing.

—To Him who is able to keep us from falling, both now and forever, thank you, God.

Sincerely,
Siera

Chapter One

Where was that little voice telling Kendall Raine she'd made the right decision? Stepping off the plane, her boots thudded onto the Key West Airport tarmac. Magical reassurance had missed the flight. The wheels were on the ground, and it was to late for second guesses. A single story terminal stood in the distance, its green roof gleaming against the clear blue April sky. Mounted on the roof, a giant statue of a family—a man, woman, and two kids welcomed her to the southernmost point of the United States. Her heart clenched. Beyond her own wits, the only person she could ever depend on was her grandma Dinah. Well, she could before her marriage. Closing her eyes, Kendall reeled her mind back to the present. She had two weeks at the Historic District Firehouse to repair some of the damage done to her career...and if she were honest, her confidence too. No distractions, no derailments. She shortened her stride as she crossed the runway. Glancing around, she eyed the thick and lush mangroves surrounding her safe haven. At the least, she welcomed the illusion of safety. If Beck ever discovered her deception...she shoved the thought out of her head. Forcing her body to relax, she inhaled deeply connecting her breathing with the elements.

The familiar heat bathing her skin reminded her of a Texas summer. A rapid replay of images detailing the life she'd left in Cockrell chilled her to the bone, making her shiver even though she wore long sleeves. With its shrinking population at four thousand strong, the small town, completely surrounded by southwest Dallas County, had been her address for three years, but the Dallas Fire and Rescue Station 58 had been her home. As one of many female firefighters on the DF&R squad she'd been a welcomed addition. *Initially.* The novelty of a woman in a male-oriented profession had worn off in the community. She hoped the same were true here at the new locale. After four years on the job, and one messy divorce, the Lord knew she needed to find a way to pick up the pieces of her life without any added drama. The wind whipped strands from the messy bun at her nape. Unsecured strands of hair snaked around her head in animated fiery waves dancing in and out of her sight. Untying the white, paisley print scarf from around her neck, she stopped to gather up the wind-generated concert playing across her head.

A woman with weathered skin wearing an orange mesh safety vest and navy blue shorts approached.

"Excuse me ma'am. We're under a severe weather watch. You have to keep moving into the terminal."

Kendall smiled, broad and wide, for the first time since she'd signed the divorce papers and left the courtroom.

"I'd be happy to keep it moving." She glanced down at her left ring finger. It was bare. She breathed in the warm, thick air with its salt and sweet palm scents, and she tasted freedom. Her mind, body, and soul felt at peace in this island paradise. The decision to save herself, regardless of the methods, had been a good one. The heavy weight that had burdened her for weeks since the divorce, finally lifted. A smile, filled with the serenity humming through her veins, formed.

"It's beautiful here," she said aloud.

"Yours is the last flight we'll get until the all-clear is issued from air traffic control," the woman called out over the dull roar of the plane's engines.

Kendall grinned as she knotted the scarf at the

back of her head. "Sorry to slow your progress."

"Honey, you're in the Conch Republic. I'd be surprised if you moved fast."

Silence reigned now that the pilots' final checks were completed. An older couple walked around Kendall. Moments later, the flight crew dressed in coordinated blue and white separates nodded to her in farewell. Yep, that was her queue to get on with her fresh start. Faces of all the people who'd made this do-over possible played in her mind. One day she'd repay Dr. Stein and his nurse, Susan, for helping her.

Her grandmother Dinah had relocated to the Keys before Kendall's marriage. Tears gathered in her eyes at the number of times she lied about a holiday visit. Beck would have never allowed her to leave the state. Driving the thirty miles to DF&R had come at a price most weeks. It was too late when she'd realized he preferred her alone, isolated.

Captain Earl Stewart, Kendall's boss at DF&R, seemed relieved when she agreed to get out of Texas. Though she never confided in him about her marital problems, he seemed to know she was in over her head with her new husband. Her true savior had come from an unlikely source. Dr. Stein had been her sounding board and a true friend. Without Gordon, she'd still be trapped in her marriage or buried in a grave. Before she'd left Dallas, she'd confided in him that she was open to his interests. There were no sparks between them, but maybe that was a good thing. Genuine friendship and respect had to be safer than love.

"Looks like you're the last one, ma'am."

"Yeah, I usually am." Beck made sure she understood and lived that truth while in his house. On his list of priorities, being last would have been too lofty a concept. Her job as a firefighter remained intact because it brought him more prestige. They were considered Cockrell's first couple of community service, akin to small town royalty.

"Don't be so hard on yourself. With all that fiery red hair and those long legs, you'll snag yourself an island cowboy in no time."

She waved away the woman's comment. Kate Fairchild, another DF&R firefighter had said the same.

"No men for me. I'm here to fight fires, that's it." The next man in her life would have to have the face of a Greek god, the body of a Roman gladiator, and enough charisma to make the First Lady skip church on Sunday morning. In fact, she planned to work like a religious zealot, keep her hair covered, and her body concealed. The scarf and over-sized sweatshirt would do the trick for now. She glanced down at her scuffed cowgirl boots. Perfect. She wanted to focus on her grandmother and her job. No boys allowed in her clubhouse.

"All I need is my rental car, my hotel room, and my engine number."

A grim expression aged the woman's face another ten years. "All the rental counters are closed because of the storm. I'm not sure about your hotel."

Kendall knew her green eyes resembled flying saucers. "Say that again."

"It's like I said. We're under a storm warning."

Kendall glanced up at the baby blue sky, eyeing a few cotton ball white clouds. With a furrowed brow she regarded the orange-vested all-knowing oracle.

The woman held up her hands, "This is the calm before the eye of the storm. Is there anyone you can call?"

"My grandmother recently moved from the Island Life Senior's Village to a beach cottage at Mile Marker 82."

That earned Kendall a pitying look.

"Honey, a magic ring, a couple of hobbits, and an

elf couldn't get you up the Keys on a day like today. And the police would turn your granny around before she hit Marathon at marker 50."

"There's no one I can call," Kendall said on a frustrated sigh.

"Call the firehouse. Those guys are used to rescuing people. Why not you?"

Oh, several reasons parked on the tip of her tongue as to why that was a bad idea. What other choices did she have? Taking her backpack off her shoulder, she unzipped the side pocket and grabbed her phone. If first impressions were everything, she was sure to fall short.

***

What kind of rock head firefighter hopped on a plane without checking the weather where he was going? Cutler Stevens turned the wheel of his GMC Canyon Extended Cab right leaving A1A as he entered the Key West Airport arrival lane. Keith Urban's "You'll Think Of Me" mixed with the smooth swish of the windshield wipers. Visibility ended ten feet in front of the hood. A storm system the size of Texas had her sights set on the Keys and Cutler had the honor of getting this dude settled before the downpour. Spying the gray clouds blanketing the horizon down to the Atlantic Ocean, he was too late. During his time in the Marine Corps, he'd done his fair share of babysitting. Some voluntarily, but most by direct order. After four years and one tour in Afghanistan, rescuing people in need was stitched in his genetic fabric. Though the thrill of automatic weapons and grenades were a distant memory, Cutler now got his adrenaline rush and satisfaction from running into the flames, saving those who couldn't save themselves, not ushering rock heads out of the storm.

The lot was devoid of cars, not even a signature Key West pink taxicab occupied the restricted lane. Once parked, Cutler tugged his baseball cap lower on his head as he stepped into the terminal. No need for this guy Kendall to see how pissed off he was at having to come out in this torrential rainspout.

Swoosh. The automated doors closed at his back. The baggage claim area was quiet, his breathing the only sound in the space. Two conveyor belts, separated by the door leading to the tarmac, sat empty. Peachy walls seemed too bright compared to the murky weather beyond the exit doors. In his steel-toe boots, he silently covered the forty by forty square foot space. Where was this guy? Maybe Cutler should check the head. Ten years after his time in uniform and he still took any responsibility, no matter how trivial, seriously. He guessed the old saying was true, "once a Marine, always a Marine". He strode past the closed rental car counters toward the door marked with the placard, 'Men'.

"Kendall," he called out. "You in there?"

"No. Wrong door."

A feminine voice, soft and husky, came from behind him. Cutler swung around and damn near stumbled over his two left feet. Eyes more verdant than a coconut palm dominated the oval face that stared up at him.

"You're Kendall Raine?" He brush stroked her with his eyes. A French vanilla complexion with just enough dark honey coloring gave her an exotic allure. Slender and toned, but also delicate with sculpted cheekbones, and a full mouth complete with a cupid's bow. Moving closer, he drank in her lean frame. Man, she had legs. Four feet of them, with a firm backside. To Cutler's six feet four inch height, Kendall was perfect for his grip. He could see tan and toned limbs riding him...stop it.

"Kendall." He breathed her name again. The sound of a sigh leaving her lips had his ears twitching like a canine with fresh prey in his sights. For a split second, the air tingled around them. He looked up, meeting the forest in springtime gaze of the beautiful woman before him. She didn't smile. Those full lips of hers thinned in warning. Thankful for small miracles, Cutler welcomed the stoic reprimand. He could already feel the chainsaw biting at his knees, threatening his wide based stance, as he ghosted over her feminine parcel again. Yep, if she flipped a grin in his direction a quartet of lumberjacks would yell *timber* because he would be going down.

"That's the name printed on my driver's license."

No smile, but a sense of humor. He liked that in a woman.

A baggy jersey knit hid whatever she was endowed with up top. Why the heck was she wearing that get-up? Even with the rain, this was still Key West. Which meant the daily forecast of eighty-degree weather could be on the return within the hour.

He extended his hand. "Cutler Stevens. I'm one of the firefighters. The captain asked me to get you settled." Which was fine when he'd thought Kendall was a man. Cutler enjoyed women. He adored women of all shapes, all sizes, and all colors. These days all his battle buddies sported double d's and thongs. He moved in and out of women's beds faster than a rolling stone. An attraction to a fellow firefighter could spell disaster for him and the team.

She placed her hand in his, and man...oh man he felt his length pulse behind his button fly jeans.

"Thanks for picking me up. I hope it wasn't out of your way."

He grinned. "It's a two by four mile island. I was close by."

She smiled in return. The softening of her facial contours moved her from beautiful to goddess territory. Snap, crackle, and then he felt the pop when the hardness in his pants began to throb. He needed away from Kendall Raine...fast.

A look down and he saw she had one suitcase besides the backpack slung over her right shoulder.

"You pack light for a woman." Maybe, she was a homebody. The luggage held one week of clothes, tops.

"I'll take that as a compliment."

He reached for her bag. "It was."

When he touched the hand she had wrapped

around the handle, she jumped. She eyed him, a wary expression on her face as she cradled her right hand like he'd burned her. How had he frightened her?

"I'm sorry," he offered, unsure what he'd done wrong. "Thought I'd carry your luggage to the truck. It's pouring. You probably want to keep your hair and stuff dry." Most women he dated would need a stiff drink if rain touched a centimeter of their skin and a tranquilizer if their hair got ruined.

"Not a problem for me." She pointed a slender finger at her head.

He frowned at the scarf covering her hair. Cutler knew women. Outside of Sunday worship, southern women didn't cover their hair. Was it a religious thing? That would explain the jumpiness and the too-big clothes. Okay, attraction averted. He respected the spiritual beliefs of others, but he liked his women willing for anything and everything. He left the holy rollers to the Bible thumpers. Cutler sinned as much as he could with every woman who would let him. His redemption came when he donned his Camo for his country, and now when he wore the blue on blue and wrapped his hands around a hose. Risking his life everyday, praying that he'd outsmart a fire...was his religion.

"Where are you staying?" he asked, all business in his tone.

"La Koncha Resort on Duval Street. Do you know where it is?"

"Yeah, tiny island, remember? Let's get out of here before the roads start to flood."

They both reached for her bag. When she wouldn't let go he tightened his grip. "I've got this, Kendall. Follow me. I'll get you there safe and sound." He felt the need to reassure her that she could count on him to keep her safe.

"I can do it myself."

Was the woman ready to do a tug-of-war over him carrying her suitcase? Growing up in the south and showing courtesy to a lady was a sign of manhood. This little Texas wildflower needed some tending and special care as a fellow firefighter, of course.

"Never doubted you could, darlin'." When he didn't relinquish the bag, reluctantly she released her grip, but her eyes remained fixed on his.

"Thanks...thank you for helping me." She hesitated. "I really appreciate it."

The sincerity in her tone shocked him. He took in her appearance again. She downplayed her beauty or at least she tried to. Even with her hair covered and the nondescript clothing, she was breathtaking. What was Kendall Raine's story? Cutler got the distinct feeling he wouldn't like it.

Chapter Two

If Cutler Stevens represented the men of Key West, thank the leaves on the trees, Kendall would be gone in two weeks. The lights in her clubhouse flickered on and the caretaker threw the doors wide open the instant she spied his firm butt covered in well-worn denim. When he turned to face her, an invisible fist grabbed the seat of her panties and ripped them off. Poof...they were gone with the wind. When the flimsy material took flight, she heard the split seams yell 'what happened'? Heck if she knew. His face, with its prominent brows and sculpted cheekbones was front page worthy, especially with those Caribbean blue eyes. A tank could hit his chiseled jaw, but she doubted that it would be moved. And his mouth, with a slightly fuller bottom lip, had an enter at your own risk warning.

Kendall tripped and stumbled across the rain-slicked pavement, worse than a college freshmen drunk on two for one shots, as she followed Cutler to his truck. Maybe if she kept her eyes off his ass...not a chance. Plump raindrops collected on her lashes.

Quick as a pair of wiper blades she wiped them away. Mother Nature would not obscure her view of the masterful creation guiding her footsteps. The man moved with the sensual grace of a king cobra weaving his way up from his lair. Hypnotic beauty to watch for any woman not on life support, but dangerous all the same. With every one of his booted footfalls thudding on the concrete, she heard the echo of his masculinity piped through ninety-inch speakers.

As they crossed the sidewalk to a he-man pickup truck tricked out in black chrome, Kendall slowed her step. She took a deep inhale, giving her mind precious seconds to process the unexpected attraction to this stranger. From this distance, she let her eyes soak in his muscles. Beneath his KWFD polo shirt and fitted jeans, a cut and conditioned warrior's body made itself known with the now damp fabric clinging to his gorgeous physique.

"How long are you in town for?" he asked. Feet still moving, Kendall answered his question, rewarding herself with another sneak peek.

"A couple of weeks," she stated. That sigh in her voice just wouldn't do. She'd taken this assignment to further her career and get her life in order. No men. Not even sexy ones with perfect smiles and super hero good looks. The real super heroes like Superman and the Hulk that got Halloween costumes and pajama sets made in their likeness.

"Our arson investigator, Nathan Zachary, was in Dallas for three months." His voice lifted against the sound of the falling precipitation. "Why are you limited to two weeks?"

She suspected Captain Stewart worried she had lost her focus. The rumors about her and Beck had died down, but when you share the same sleeping quarters in twenty-four hour shifts, people talk. Sending her to Key West was a test. How broken was she? The itch to push the limit had to be put back in the bottle if she wanted to stay on the DF&R squad. Could she control the inner darkness her time with Beck had unearthed? Kendall didn't ponder the answer to that question. She had lost her parents, her belief in the sanctity of marriage, and her faith that when confronted with an injustice, the people around her would intervene. She could have choked on her naivety. Nothing else would be taken from her...not without one hell of a fight.

"Assignments are not created equal." Kendall arched a brow in defiance.

Cutler's ocean blue collared shirt fit him to

perfection. Wind blew the rain at them sideways, making the fabric cling to his chiseled flank on the left and billow outward on the right. The denim jeans hugged his tight butt. She traced the outline of his muscled thighs down to his ripped and shredded calf muscles. Instead of a firefighter calendar, his body should be photoshopped on every anti-depressant prescription bottle. She certainly felt happier since he'd arrived.

But wait, there's more she heard the voice in her head say. His blond hair flowed in thick waves to just shy of his shoulders. It wasn't that uni-shade of blond from a bottle either, nope. His mane consisted of layered dark strands with golden ropes beneath sun-lightened waves. The ends were saturated with rainwater and she noticed the curl pattern had deepened. With those blue eyes, the body designed by a god, and the storm on the horizon, she half expected a trident to appear in his hand and the rain to obey his command. Definitely, Olympic God material.

"Kendall."

Her breath hitched when he called her name. Unfortunately her brain was preoccupied with shoveling coal into her long dormant sexual furnace so Kendall didn't stop her feet's forward advance. She continued on the horny bunny train to X-ratedville until she slammed into his back. The air swooshed from her lungs. Her right foot slipped and she felt her knee buckle. In an effort to break her impending fall, she grabbed Cutler around the waist, plastering her front to his back. Dang, his ass was rock hard and she melted into his backside like butter on hot breakfast toast.

A muscled forearm came down over hers, locking her in place. The heat from his palm, broad and callused, warmed her wet skin.

He chuckled. "Grabby little thing, aren't you." For a moment they both stood still. "I like it."

Her head rested on his back. Slowly, remnants of proper manners invaded her conscious thought and she moved to pull her arm free of his.

"It was an accident...sorry." Seconds ticked by in silence. Would he accept her apology? People bumped into one another everyday, of course he would accept her apology. She realized the fantasy musings combined with an active imagination had her overreacting. So, why hadn't he said anything?

Cutler's fingers tightened on her arms and her skin started to sizzle at the added contact.

"You getting caught watching my ass or you hugging it?"

She was speechless. What kind of man brought up his assets with a woman he'd just met? Kendall swallowed her retort because...excitement fluttered her insides, not remorse.

"Which is it darlin'? Accidentally watching or accidentally hugging?"

They both were looking forward. Her front pressed against his back, so he couldn't see her expression. Did she want him to see the sparkle of lust in her eyes? Nope...she had to stay focused or at least make it to her hotel before she had any more *thoughts about her new teammate.*

"I think we should go, Cutler."

She had to avoid engaging this man. In a matter of minutes, he and his sinful good looks had disarmed her. What would happen if she surrendered to her cravings?

"Why...I'm trying my best to be hospitable."

She became aware of him stroking her skin. Goosebumps. Yep, and then she started to tremble. Kendall felt the subtle shift of muscle along his back.

"You okay?" His voice held a hint of concern.

She lifted her head and looked up. From over his

left shoulder, Cutler stared down at her, a furrow between his brows. He must think her a brazen woman. She'd been caught checking him out, there was no denying that fact. She lowered her head not wanting him to see the lust firing behind her eyes. Maybe Beck's accusations about her nature held some merit. *Kendall Raine, you are one messed up public servant, girlfriend.*

Cutler turned around. She realized she still held him around the waist. Real careful like, she unlaced her fingers from behind his back. In a parallel universe, she could separate herself from her very nice co-worker and he would do her a solid and pretend he didn't notice.

"Leave them there, darlin'."

She froze. Oh gosh, would he lecture her, and then tell her new boss she was a touchy flake with a wandering eye.

"I'm sorry, Cutler. My attention was...," she trailed off. Her attention and her thoughts were in the gutter, rolling around with thighs wide enough for his tapered hips.

She gasped when he pulled her in tighter. "Your body just softened in my arms, darlin'. Tell me what you're thinking about us right now." The look on his face was somewhere between a smile and a frown. "I doubt you're sorry about touching me. We're both adults, so you don't have to deny yourself a damn thing, Kendall."

Her stomach fluttered at the musical hum he added to each syllable. What was she sorry for again? Not a darn thing when he said her name with that slow drawl. Her heart thundered in her chest at their closeness.

"I...I ah, I ah." She hesitated. Nope, that was not hesitation, she was stuttering. Th-Th-Th-Th—, That's all folks.

His fingertips sat in the small of her back. She gasped when he pressed deeper into the tissue making small circles. The sensual pull overwhelmed her sexual hibernation. Her libido burst from its cell like the Incredible Hulk, angry with pent up frustration, and powerful enough to tackle Cutler if she didn't put some space between them. Of course, with his chest pressing into hers, her body responded in kind. Her breasts became hypersensitive, her nipples tightened, pushing back against his packed muscle.

"Kendall."

Her name was more of a question on his lips. She

closed her eyes. How had she allowed this to happen?

"Yes." She held her breath, wondering what he would say next.

He cleared his throat before he spoke. "You're responding."

Okay, this was not the conversation she needed to have with the guy giving her a ride. A woman, even a divorced one with experience, did not discuss nipple behavior with a stranger. A stranger that lit a fire where there had been dry ice. Very ouch.

"Let's pretend none of this ever happened," she said on a shaky breath.

"Won't work for me." He lowered his head. The stubble covering his jaw brushed across her cheek and she felt a pulse of desire deep in her core. His scent was that of a cool ocean breeze mixed with spring rain. Both had always felt heavenly on her bare skin. He would too, Kendall thought.

"Why not?" she croaked.

He took her chin between his thumb and forefinger, capturing her gaze.

"Because I never lie to myself and I won't ever lie to you." Cutler closed the distance between them, damp bodies touching. He whispered in her ear, "Now, do you want me darlin' or is this your normal reaction when a man is in close proximity?"

Kendall gasped. What woman went super nova around every guy? Once again, she chastised herself for lack of focus. She needed to shut him down...now. Right after she got her body under control.

"I don't want anybody," she snapped.

"Unless you've got some nervous system damage, that's not true. You want me."

She grumbled, but told him the truth. "If I did, I don't want to want you. You happy now?" she ground out, not pleased at the direction of her welcome to Key West conversation.

"Not one bit, because" he said dropping his hands from her waist and grabbing her wrist, "if you do want me, I need to get you to your hotel ASAP."

Mental whiplash had her brain scrambling to catch up. She told him the truth, now she was public enemy number one. "What's the rush?"

"Besides the storm brewing? Us getting involved would be a disaster."

"I already told you, I don't want to want you."

"Darlin', that there's a giant red flag with the words, 'aim here' printed on both sides."

"You'd pursue me anyway?" she asked, disbelief in her tone.

"I love the hunt, Kendall, but I'm a one-night at a time kinda guy and we have to work together."

"Are you implying I'd get hooked on you?"

His eyes raked up and down her body, a wicked grin covering his lips. "I'd try my hardest to make it so."

Instantly, her insides heated. She forced herself to look away.

"We need to stay away from one another, Kendall."

When her stomach quivered in response, she nodded in agreement. Her phone chimed an incoming message. She glanced down at the smart watch on her wrist. It was Gordon. She was sure the doctor wanted to ensure she'd arrived safely in Key West. She let the call go to voicemail. Kendall glanced over at Cutler. Hot, burning lust licked through her veins. The sooner Cutler dropped her off at the hotel the better. Her feet were on the ground, but clearly, her head was in the clouds.

Chapter Three

Cutler glanced around the empty La Koncha Hotel lobby. Its black and white decor elegant, but too stark for Kendall's colorful personality. He was having a major problem keeping his erection in the down position. In the two-mile drive from the airport, everything in him wanted to put her on a tray table with him pinning her in the upright position. He needed to get a grip, and the front desk clerk, with his bored expression, did little to help the situation.

"What do you mean you cancelled her reservation?" Cutler struggled to keep his voice calm. He felt on edge around Kendall, an emotion he rarely experienced with women.

"Cutler...please," Kendall said tugging at his shirt sleeve. "I could try and reach my Grandma Dinah again."

He glanced down at her. Those bright green eyes of hers brought him to heel like a match to a flame. A couple of dial backs on the testosterone might help him approach the problem with a level head. Who was he kidding? One look at Kendall had him aching to take her in his arms. She'd tried to reach her granny twice during the ride. With the storm barreling up the coast, Cutler wasn't surprised that some areas had already lost connectivity.

"You're safer here." Not necessarily with him. "The middle Keys are less populated with less support services. It could be days before power is restored."

The clerk looked up from his computer monitor. The sudden rise of the man's shoulders told Cutler whatever he would say next would not be helpful.

"Everything is closed or closing, sir. The hotel has evacuated its guests and cancelled all pending reservations including Ms. Raine's."

A touch to his forearm drew his attention. "Cutler, just drop me off at the station. I'll bunk there for the night."

He shook his head. "The Captain called in two crews just in case. There's nowhere for you to sleep."

She gave him a wry smile. "I don't suppose there's a shelter nearby?"

A twinge of annoyance thumped in his chest. He'd never leave a woman he was responsible for at a shelter.

Taking her hand he led them back to the

revolving doors. "I know someone who can help us."

Five minutes later Cutler walked through the doors of Hobo Alley Bar and Grill, the local firefighter favorite.

"You hang out at a place called Hobo Alley?" Kendall teased, following him inside.

The soothing melody of a country crooner hit Cutler's eardrums and his heart rate slowed to a waltz. The sweet smell of barley, hops, and fried corn wafted past his nose and he inhaled, pulling the familiar fragrance deeper inside. This was his home away from home.

"Darlin' the only things that separate a saltwater Conch from a real Hobo, is a paycheck and a boat. Otherwise, we're indistinguishable."

Voices drifted up from tables and he didn't have to look to know who was talking. A table full of old timers called his name in unison. Cutler tipped the bill of his cap in greeting.

"Gentlemen."

"Yea, on what planet?" came the retort, followed by some hearty laughter.

"Guess he's trying to impress the new lady," someone shouted.

Kendall laughed behind him. "How often are you

here?" she inquired.

Hobo Alley, a favorite with the local bubbas and cuzzies, was nothing fancy to look at, but the camaraderie he deemed priceless. The place had a rustic feel with dark plank floors and wooden tables. It sat on the corner of Eaton and Key West's infamous Duval Street. Twin windows the size of mansion doors faced south toward Truman Annex with a matching pair pointed east toward the Atlantic Ocean. In addition to the primo street view, there was a room-length bar, a band, and one hot plate dinner special every night.

"Every chance I get," Cutler laughed.

Scuffed high top tables loaded down with empty amber colored bottles filled the room. The Key West firefighters had a designated table at Hobo's. Rachel, the redhead that owned the place, called it the hot guys' table. The Captain had outdone himself with the recall roster, every bar stool stood empty. Cutler thought he'd dodged a bullet with the storm falling on his Kelly Days, a four-day vacation following his forty-eight on/seventy-two hours off rotation.

Trace Fletcher, a member of his fire crew, was exiting the blue door, marked cowboys.

"Trace, man. Am I glad to see you." Trace was

the biggest SOB on the island at six feet five inches, packing two eighty on a light day. Ink black hair and eyes added to his intimidation factor, but the guy had a heart of gold double his body weight for everyone he met. His two-bedroom condo was nestled on Key West's only golf course and with its ensuite bath layout it would be perfect for an overnight guest. Cutler could supply Kendall with enough food, water, and candles, and then check on her after the storm. Temptation out of sight, would hopefully translate to trashy thoughts out of mind.

"Don't be too glad, I'm headed into the station to relieve the day crew."

Cutler slapped him on the back. "That's perfect because, our new firefighter," he reached for Kendall and she stumbled backwards. Both men regarded the woman in their midst.

Kendall stepped up. "Hi, Trace. I'm Kendall Raine, here on temp assignment from Dallas Fire & Rescue."

Trace took her hand in his. Cutler felt a knot form in his gut when Kendall gave the other man a generous smile.

"So, you're at the Historic District Firehouse with Cutler?" she asked.

"For now. I'm training to be an arson investigator, but we already have Nathan as the primary on any suspicious cases. I should be headed your way in a few months. Maybe you can show me around Dallas when I arrive."

Cutler cleared his throat, not liking how comfortable the conversation flowed between his friend and the woman that had his Levi's fitting like nut crushers.

"Kendall needs to crash at your place. The hotel cancelled her reservation."

Trace frowned. "No can do, Cut. The guys that live up the Keys had first dibs. Even the kitchen floor will have a sleeping bag. Wish I could help."

Trace pivoted. "Sorry, Kendall."

"It's okay, Trace," she said, placing a light touch to his arm.

Cutler ground his teeth. She flinched if he came near her, but the beast got a feel-me-up. Okay, maybe he was exaggerating, but she hadn't touched him willingly. The whole 'break her fall' thing at the airport didn't count.

"Be safe, man. I'll hit you up in a couple of days," Cutler said before Trace walked off.

Kendall tilted her head, her gaze following Trace

as he exited the bar. What kind of game was she playing? First him, now Trace had her attention. His gut twisted. Cutler thought of his mom, how she used to lead his dad around by the nose. A manipulative woman would never enthrall him.

"He seems nice."

Cutler grunted at Kendall's assessment.

Spying Claudia, a permanent fixture since the bar's foundation, Cutler signaled the waitress over. "The crowd seems thin tonight."

Her beehive bobbled with the animated moves of a living, breathing entity as she spoke.

"That's because the boss called this last round."

He hated asking anyone to take on a complete stranger, but he barely had control of his libido. "I need a favor."

"Name it, suga'. You know you're family around here."

That's what Cutler loved about Hobo's. It was more than a bar by design. Rachel and her staff treated their customers like family.

He pulled Kendall from behind his back where she'd listened intently, but remained silent.

"Kendall's a new firefighter in town and she needs a place to hunker down for the storm."

Claudia, at five foot seven, glanced up at Kendall. "Nice to meet you, Kendall, and welcome to Hobo Alley."

Kendall laughed and his sex hardened...again. Thank the sweet baby Savior he would be leaving her in Claudia's capable hands.

"Not welcome to Key West, but welcome to the bar?"

"The Keys have a way of creating a unique welcome for each of us. At Hobo Alley, everyday is the same. Good booze, good music, great food, and fantastic people. Next time I see you, suga' you tell me about our Key West welcome."

Kendall stole a look at him, and then turned away. A hint of pink tinted her cheeks beneath her warmed honey skin.

Cutler took a seat. He watched as Kendall instantly warmed to Claudia's southern wisdom.

"I'll do just that. So, I'm going home with you, I guess?"

"Nope." Claudia grinned. "I already have a bed warmer, if you know what I mean."

He jumped to his feet. "Well, what was all that talk about family for, then?"

"Since you're family I can be honest with you,"

she smirked. "I don't have the space. Ask Rachel, maybe she has room at her place."

He scowled and strode toward the bar where Rachel stood watching his approach with a raised brow. The scrape of Kendall's boots strutting in step with his met his ears. They reached the bar at the same time with Rachel standing behind the wooden counter.

"Hey, Cutler. What can I do you for?"

Thunder rumbled all around them, the bottles littered throughout the establishment rattled a discordant chime. A crack of lighting flashed close by, the illumination similar to a camera flash bulb reflecting in all the glass panes separating Hobo's from the outside world. Rachel's dark eyes danced with merriment, her fire engine red hair giving her the appearance of a Valkyrie.

"Hi, I'm Kendall Raine and Cutler wants you to take me off his hands."

Cutler tried not to wince when Rachel tossed him a disapproving glare.

"You look harmless," Rachel mused.

Kendall stiffened at his side. Out of the corner of his eye he regarded her. The pulse at her neck jumped in an erratic beat. What was up with this woman? One minute she laughed and joked, and the next she looked ready to do battle. He could read her change in mood, but he didn't understand the cause.

Cutler ran his fingers through his hair, puzzling out the best approach to getting Kendall home with Rachel.

"I didn't say she was dangerous."

The woman fancied herself a matchmaker. His best friend, Nathan, had met his wife, Symphony Porter at Hobo Alley. She was the waitress at their table Nathan's first night back in town from Dallas Fire and Rescue. For weeks, Cutler had tried to gain Symphony's affections. One look at Nathan and she'd hitched her wagon to the investigator. Even though, Nathan had arrested her under suspicion of arson, somehow they still made it to the altar and were expecting their first child.

"As long as you're not in harm's way, Cutler, Kendall can go home with you."

Sure he had enough supplies at his place, but stuck in the house with Kendall for possibly two days was the opposite of safe. His hospitality stopped at sleepovers with his fellow female firefighter who had a body made for wrapping around a man.

"Ah...I'm willing to sleep here in the bar,"

Kendall said.

Cutler let his annoyance show. "You're not staying in the bar alone and sleeping on the floor."

She shrugged. "I've slept in worse."

"Not on my watch."

The three of them fell silent. Rachel was up to something. He glanced at Kendall, wondering if she felt the undercurrents flowing between them. Why was he so in tune to this woman? He didn't believe for a minute that she wanted to stay in the bar alone during a storm. He sensed a sadness in her. Was she upset that he was trying to get rid of her? He looked at her, taking in her impassive expression. If he took her home could he keep his hands off her? They were about to find out.

"Come on, let's go home," he heard himself say.

Kendall's eyes flashed with pleasure. He found he liked seeing her happy. Had she worried he'd leave her stranded?

They were almost to the door when Rachel called his name.

"Your future is full of surprises that your past will help you claim, Cutler."

Kendall leaned into him. "What does that mean?"

"It means Rachel is playing fairy godmother again. We're stuck together for the next two days, and I'm going to need a lot of cold showers."

"I can stay out of your way. I won't make anything hard for you, Cutler."

He took her by the elbow as they exited the bar and walked out in the storm.

"It already is."

Chapter Four

Cutler's place was cozy and masculine. A futon sofa sat in the middle of the room. A cross-section of an oak tree with a heavy layer of clear varnish served as the coffee table. Mega was too small of a word to describe the television.

"The bedroom is to the right. It's the only one, so you'll sleep there. I'll take the couch."

Was he for real? Beck would never make a sacrifice for her comfort. What would Cutler's kindness cost her later?

Mind still whirling from his kind gesture, Kendall reveled in her seemingly good luck of the draw. So much of her life had gone wrong in the past three years.

"Your eyes are beautiful," she heard him say.

Just that simple compliment put her on alert. Would he demand she strip for him now? Adrenaline spiked in her blood stream. Or would he try to shove her down to her knees before him? She'd rather spend the night in jail, after the cops hauled her away for punching him in the biscuits, before she did either.

"They glow with the slightest act of kindness."

"Kindness is a gift, Cutler."

And there she was, happy he'd brought her home and offered up his bed. Indeed, it was a good deed from a good man.

"I'm not arguing the point, but—"

Kendall glanced over her shoulder, not wanting to hear him say anything to undo the magic.

"You mind if I hang out in here on the couch for a little while?" She needed open space. After the flight in a tin can-sized airplane and the truck ride, the bedroom could wait.

Cutler lifted his hat from his head, ruffled his hair, and wiggled the cap back into place. Why was it everything he did turned her to putty? It was just hair. Hair she wanted to run her fingers through, as he...stop it.

"Sure thing, Kendall."

He reached for her suitcase...again. What was with him and carrying her luggage? After three years of marriage to Beck, she could even have sex by herself. Something she'd never imagined would be her fate as a new bride.

"I can do it, Cutler."

Cutler pulled both hands back and jammed them into his pockets. "There's no doubt in my mind that you can take care of yourself, but while you're in my home, I'm asking you to let me help."

Gosh, was she being that difficult? Did he see her as some ultra feminist that was so focused on proving her independence that she refused help from a man? Before she'd met Beck, having a man assist her with her chair or a door had been flattering. During her marriage, she'd learned through blood, bruises, and broken bones that accepting anything came at a cost. Refusing anything carried a higher toll.

Lifting the bag, she hesitated before handing it to him. "Thank you...for everything."

Taking the bag he gave her a roguish grin in exchange. "My pleasure," he said, raking down her body in a leisurely eye patrol.

"Is there anything else I can help you with?"

A groan was on the tip of her tongue. She thought they had agreed to play nice.

"Behave." *Please...because I want to be so bad with you.*

"Why...being naughty is much more fun."

That earned him a stern glower, which he responded to with a teasing grin. He snagged her backpack from her shoulder and carried both bags toward her bedroom for the night.

Against her better judgment Kendall watched the graceful glide of his masculine frame. "I thought we both agreed us hooking up was a bad idea."

He paused, catching her in his languid blue stare, "We did, but I never promised I would stop trying to change your mind."

Lust heated his eyes and she curled her fingers into fists, pressing her nails into her palms, and nailing her feet in place. That ocean breeze scent that was uniquely Cutler's seemed to flare like a fire that had located a new energy source, beckoning her to walk into his arms. He waited a heartbeat, and then he was gone. When he disappeared behind the partially open door, she grabbed the back of the futon to steady herself. It was obvious she wanted him. Would he push her to give in? What would he do if she didn't? She felt Beck's hand close around her throat, the weight of his bulky body pinning her down.

"Hey...Kendall..." Cutler stood in the doorway, the space made narrow by his broad shoulders. His voice held a whisper of concern a second before he moved in her direction.

She drug her eyes up. They locked with his. He must have registered the rising sense of panic churning inside her because he stopped dead in his tracks.

"You okay?"

She swallowed her mental rankings. He'd only shown her kindness and it was unfair of her to project old records onto a new player, but...she had to ask.

"Cutler are you sure it's safe for me to be here alone with you?" Her thoughts were scattered. If he were dependent on Kendall's self control, they would be in bed together before the stroke of midnight.

He stared at her, his brows pulled low over his eyes. "I joke around a lot, Kendall, but I wouldn't take anything you didn't offer first. You feel me?"

Oh, he remained across the room, but she felt him. And could smell him, and the rake of his touch against her skin sent shivers up her spine, like back at the airport terminal.

"I feel you," she whispered.

He studied her. His posture that of a hunter sizing up its prey. There was not one physical characteristic about this man that said, *I'm a safe haven for troubled women.* Quite the opposite in fact. when Kendall regarded his wickedly handsome features and the body belonging to a god, she was sure everything about Cutler Stevens spelled trouble for most females.

"I bet you do." He walked past her. "Have a seat while I cook us up some dinner."

She breathed easy. "I could help," she chimed in.

"Nope, you stay right there and keep feeling me."

"That's not what I meant, Cutler."

"Oh, darlin', you are a terrible liar."

Beck used to say the same thing before he closed their bedroom door, trapping her inside with him.

***

Cutler's kitchen was small, but modern with oak and glass cabinets, brushed nickel hardware, and twin enamel sinks.

A dinette set would dwarf the space, so two wooden stools with cushioned seats were parked opposite the kitchen at the Travertine counter. He'd cooked several dishes just in case they lost electrical power during the night. He wanted Kendall to have a full dinner and breakfast. Platters with eggs, bacon strips, baked chicken tenders, and broiled Hogfish filets with sliced potatoes, the local island favorite, covered the counter top. He pulled a bag of broccoli from the microwave and a wooden bowl with a spinach salad from the fridge.

"Wow," Kendall said staring at the mini-feast. "How many people are you expecting to ride the storm out with us?"

"I like to be prepared. I have a Yeti cooler stocked with drinks and plenty of ice. I can keep you well-fed if we loose power." He could keep her satisfied in a number of ways if she'd let down her guard.

Cutler wiped his hands on the plaid dishtowel buttoned to the oven door handle. "Make yourself a plate. I want to stock your room with a couple of flashlights, a few jar candles, and a crank-powered radio."

"You've thought of everything, Jim Cantori."

Cutler laughed. "Those guys on the Weather Channel only have a Parka and a microphone. At least let me be one of the Storm Chasers with a crew, equipment, and a camera."

He could definitely envision them in a man versus nature scenario. Protecting her soft curves from the elements, maybe a few scrapes he could kiss the ouch away...or rub the ache from—. His name on her lips disrupted Cutler's thoughts. He shook his head, clearing his motherboard...not really. Had Kendall noticed the direction of his thoughts? He glanced in her direction. Lips glistened with moisture, her pulse jumped in her neck, and she was holding her breath. Heck yeah she'd noticed, and was in the eye of the storm with him. Awareness and desire sparked between them.

"Fine, you win," Kendall blurted out.

He'd relaxed a hip against the counter, studying her. Her eyes widened at the bulge in his jeans.

"Do those wandering eyes of yours mean I'm going to get lucky?"

"Nope, nope," she insisted. "You're luck has run out in that department." She threw her hands up and took a step backwards.

He shrugged. "You know...hands up generally means you've surrendered." He grinned when she gasped. "Be back in a minute, darlin'. Plates are in the cabinet next to the stove."

Cutler didn't wait. Instead he collected the hurricane supplies as Kendall oriented herself to the kitchen, gathering plates and utensils for two. Though the storm wasn't predicted to reach hurricane strength winds, his preparations would work in any scenario.

"Hmm," came from the kitchen.

He looked up from the console beneath the television when she didn't say anything further.

"You need something?" he called out.

"Surprisingly, no."

Her voice sounded far away. Was she shocked to find a bachelor with a full compliment of kitchen accessories?

"Did you expect paper plates, a chipped mug, and a fridge full on longnecks?"

"I admit, the well organized cabinets and the set of everyday china caught me off guard."

With supplies in hand, he stood and strode to the closed bedroom door along the same wall. "I'm thirty-two, not twenty-two."

She gestured to her heart. "I meant no disrespect. Count it to my head, not my heart."

"I'd accept a kiss as a first step toward an apology."

She laughed. It was the sweetest sound to his ears. He sensed Kendall hadn't laughed a lot in her life.

"Get over it, cowboy."

Smiling she continued to fumble in the cabinets, not looking at him.

"You wound me, darlin'."

"As if I ever could."

He stared at the crown of her head as she bent over an empty plate. Cutler knew she had the power to hurt him, even though she wouldn't let him get close. Maybe, it was because she kept him at a distance when others never had.

When he joined her at the counter, there were two plates loaded down with a little of everything he'd prepared. She'd made his plate. When was the last time a woman that he brought home had prepared a plate for him?

He stared at her. Who was Kendall Raine, really? Even his friend's wives didn't make their husband's plate. "Thanks."

"You're welcome." She gave him a shy smile and he suspected she drew pleasure from caring for him, even if it was in a small way.

Kendall claimed one of the stools at the counter, but Cutler hesitated.

"What..." she said, with a fork full of salad suspended in mid-air. "Is it okay for me to sit here?"

He felt like a heel. He wanted her to be

comfortable with him. "Sure...it's just, I usually eat in front of the television."

He wanted her to join him. It would feel weird to have her at his back. Him facing the tube and her staring at the stove.

"I could join you, if you'd like?"

Why did she seem so hesitant, like he had to approve her every move?

"That would be great."

Initially, they ate in companionable silence. She had to be the first woman he'd met that didn't chat up the quiet with the person sitting next to her. Refusing to force her to talk, Cutler grabbed the television remote from the rotating holder on the floor and pressed on.

Sports Center's Chris Berman's voice filled the room. He was prepared to turn the channel, when the she spoke.

"Can't believe Cleveland lost that game."

Cutler nearly dropped his plate. If Kendall Raine was a sports lover, he was in real danger of falling hard.

"You like sports?"

"Just basketball, football, and baseball."

He grinned. "Woman, you're a keeper."

She laughed. "You're so easy."

"You have no idea," he teased. In fact, during the course of their conversation it had gotten easier for him to stay *hard*.

The food and the beers kept flowing. Before long, he and Kendall were laughing and she even gave him a couple of play-punches to the arm. They both were Dallas Cowboy fans. When he mentioned Tampa Bay and the Jacksonville Jaguars that earned him the third arm punch of the evening.

"To prove how diehard I am, me and Trace take the Fort Myers ferry, get a rental car, and drive to Tampa Bay at least twice a year. You're welcome to join us."

"Wow," her voice climbed an octave. "I haven't attended a live game since before my marriage."

"How can that be?" he quizzed. "You live in Dallas and you don't go to the games?"

Kendall drew her lip between her teeth. "It's a long, ugly story."

"You want to tell me about it?"

Her emerald eyes constricted like the power being cut to a vintage television screen fading to black.

"Nope, and I don't think I'll be around long

enough for any ferry rides."

He wanted her to confide in him. Man, he wanted her to feel safe with his touch.

"You could stay longer, right?" Why had he asked that question? He'd only met her a few hours earlier. The attraction he felt could be fleeting.

She stared at her hands, and then back up at him. Her eyes looked haunted. Had she been thinking the same as him?

"I need another beer," he said coming to his feet. And a hole in his head to drain out the stupid.

Chapter Five

Cutler sank down onto the futon next to her, just as Kendall finished her second plate. Booted feet propped on the stump that doubled as furniture gave her a premium view of his muscular legs. Gosh, he was sexy, even when he wasn't trying.

"You were hungry for bacon and eggs." Laughter glinted in his eyes.

She rubbed her full belly. "Breakfast foods do it for me."

Without asking, he grabbed both their plates and headed toward the kitchen. Thank goodness...because his nearness was doing it for her, too. Excavating the food on the counter helped to keep her hands busy and... To. Herself.

Jumping up, she scooped up their empty beer bottles. When was the last time she had sat and ate a meal, drank a few beers with a man and not been terrified a blow would land on her arm or chest for some unknown offense? The comfortable companionship reminded her of the lonely existence she led. After the meal Cutler had prepared for them and the conversation, the least she could do was load the dishwasher.

His galley kitchen design meant with the both of them trying to help the other, it was going to be a tight fit.

"I would've gotten everything cleaned up, Kendall. You're a guest in my home."

He didn't look at her like a guest. All those stolen looks had her hormones jumping like a disco.

"Yea, I know, but I ate enough for three people."

Cutler encouraged her to eat. Beck would have taken her plate and tossed it in the trash if he decided 'too much' food covered her plate.

"Three ladies, maybe, but not more than me and the guys when I cook down at the station."

"And here I was thinking I was special." She grinned, loading the last pot into the bottom rack.

"You are," he said, turning so that they faced each other. "You got a little sauce on your cheek."

From out of nowhere, she saw a hand moving toward her face. A part of her brain knew she was far away from Beck, but on reflex, she threw her hands up, shielding her face from a blow.

She had gotten too comfortable. In this tight space, it would be hard to defend herself, but she would inflict as much damage as possible before she went down. There were knives in a kitchen block to her left.

"Kendall?" Anger had tightened Cutler's voice.

An alarm rang in her head. Run, it said. God, she knew that tone better than she wanted to. She'd been trained to fear those subtle changes. Tremors racked her body. Why had she come home with this man? For heaven's sake, how many bruises and broken bones did it take until she got the message? Cutler stepped closer and she jumped, unable to control the response.

"Lower your arms, darlin'." His voice was softer, no... Tender was a better word.

Inhaling, she breathed in deep, searching for the control she had surrendered too quickly. When nothing happened, she released the tension in her upper body and dropped her arms to her side.

Those blue eyes of his held her captive.

"I've never hit a woman in my life. I won't hurt you. Your defensive posturing every ten minutes makes me want to murder the asshat that made you scared for me to touch you."

She lifted her chin. "That's an easy enough fix. Keep your hands to yourself."

A tick started along his jaw.

"Look, Kendall. I'm a lot of things, but a liar isn't on the list. I wanted to touch you the moment I saw you. That hasn't changed, but you know that, don't you?"

She opened her mouth, but she stopped herself when he twisted those *just enough fullness to be perfect* lips into a frown.

"I know it's a bad idea for us to become involved. That's why I dragged us both to that hotel, and then to Hobo Alley. Having you under my roof is a temptation I don't need."

She didn't care for him labeling her the cause for his wayward libido. "Well, I don't need a grown and sexy cowboy juicing me up, either."

A broad smile revealing all his pearly whites spread across his chiseled features.

"How juicy are we talking?"

Heat crept up her neck. As the spread of warmth registered internally before infusing her cheeks, he began to laugh.

"I'm not answering that."

"You look like you could use another beer. There's a few left along with a bottle of wine in the fridge."

Cutler reached for her hand and she stiffened. He growled in frustration. Pulling the cap from his head, he tossed it in the direction of the futon. It landed soundlessly on the giant cushion.

"What the hell did he do to you?"

"I don't want to talk about what you think you know about my life." He ignored her comment.

She'd left her memories of her marriage along with her signature on a divorce decree. Freedom and her life was her share of their martial assets. Beck was more than happy when she gave him the house, the cars, and the five figures in their bank account. If she'd taken anything, he'd have had a reason to come looking for her.

"Since you're not wearing a ring, I assume it was an ex-lover."

She shrugged, hoping it would end this conversation.

"He hit you more than once."

Kendall didn't retreat, but she was old enough not to be baited into discussing her marriage with a stranger...albeit, a handsome, wildly tempting stranger.

They stared each other down.

When he saw she wasn't joining him in this

conversation, he relaxed his stance, propping a booted foot on the wall at his back.

"Probably for some minor offense. Am I right?"

She scoffed at him. "I had no idea I'd be spending the next two days with a prophet, so you tell me," she said, hands on her hips.

He grimaced. "It doesn't take divine intervention or a psychology degree to see if you touch me you're fine, but if I touch you, you darn near jump out of your skin."

She was done here. "Just because we're stuck together doesn't mean you get to cut me open to see how I tick."

He pushed away from the wall. "I don't cut and I don't hit," he rasped.

Fine, he was one of the good ones. He'd be great for some equally great beach bombshell. "You said I could use your room, right?"

All his golden boy charm seemed to evaporate. His face went blank. His cool regard gave her the impression she had disappointed him. Grab a number and get in line.

"Yea, I need to change the sheets."

She pushed away from the dishwasher and made for the bedroom door. "Don't worry about it. I'll sleep in my clothes."

"Why? Is it too much of a temptation to have my scent on your skin?"

The words were cold and biting. Just a few hours together, and she'd irritated him. Beck would have left her with a carefully placed bruise for less.

"I need to focus on my job and my family. And for the record, I caught your scent, cowboy." Every breath drew Cutler Stevens closer to her heart. The silly organ caused too much trouble.

***

Cutler lay still on the futon staring at the ceiling. Midnight had come and gone, along with the electrical power. He assumed Kendall slept through the pop and sizzle of the transformer fireworks. Rain beat against the house, the sound louder than a thousand marbles rushing through a rip in a bag. Wind howled and roared as lighting illuminated the sky.

He needed to get over his fascination with Kendall. The woman was focused on her career and spending time with her grandmother. Though he'd had a great evening with her, did she feel the same way about him?

The sound of a lightning strike split the air, and then the ground and the house shook. The smell of burnt wood filled the air, the pungent scent pouring in through the vents. All of that brought him up off his bed for the night, but it was Kendall's ear-piercing scream that had him leaping across the table and sprinting to his bedroom.

"Kendall," he yelled.

When she didn't reply, and the door remained closed, he hit the panel with his shoulder, pushing the thing wide.

What he saw had his stomach plummeting to his feet. Flashbacks of his time in combat stormed his brain like a recon force on a covert mission.

Kendall stood, a naked fire goddess, with a gun pointed at his chest. Why the heck would she pull a firearm? And why, oh why, did he take a step closer?

He couldn't take his eyes off her. She was beautiful. With each flash of lightning, her body glowed in the darkness; her bare shoulders, the rise and fall of her full breasts with each breath, abs so flat he could lick a straight line to...His eyes traveled lower to the close-trimmed triangle between her legs. Cutler's throat went dry, his mouth watered, and he was thirsty all at once.

"You're a natural red." He some how pushed the words past his strangled breath. Talk about a smoking hot, naked gun.

"I have a gun pointed at you, but you're more concerned with my bare essentials?"

This remarkable woman, unashamed of her nakedness and confident in her ability to protect stirred Cutler's blood like none other. He grinned, moving closer still.

"Darlin', I'm a former Marine. Guns in the bedroom could be considered foreplay." Now, he leaned in close, the heat of her body as he entered her personal space was a beacon for his erection. "If I let you shoot me, will you put your mouth where I tell you?"

He saw the pulse in her slender neck quicken. The blood in his veins heated to a slow, rolling boil. He watched her green eyes darken to a velvet forest, rich and intoxicating, and then they dilated. Hmm, she liked to play on the edge...so did he.

"Cutler." She cocked her head, her finger tightening on the trigger. "Keep your eyes up here cowboy and tell me what was that sound?"

Cutler didn't hesitate to slip into his staff

sergeant role at the heightened state of alert in her voice. "Lower your weapon, Kendall."

"No, tell me who's outside," she said pulling a white flimsy shirt over her head with one hand while maintaining her grip on the gun with the other.

He got the sense she had experience firing a gun.

"First, put the gun down. Then tell me why the heck you're naked in my bed without me."

"The bed smells like you and I tried to settle into sleep, but I kept...sniffing and...," she trailed off.

Was she insane? She had no idea how close she was to danger being butt naked under his roof. His resistance was hair trigger sensitive when she was clothed, for sure he was a goner now that he'd seen her goodies.

"So you decided letting it all hang out and rollin' around in my man spice would make it easier for you?"

She grunted as if he were the crazy one.

"No, the clothes were irritating...so I took everything off."

He could envision her plump breasts rubbing against his sheets, the nipples erect and hyper-responsive to the touch. Her feminine flesh swollen and puffy, ready for him to take full possession. With the loose fit of his shorts, maybe she hadn't noticed his shaft bobbing in agreement.

"Darlin' if you're itching for the real thing, I'm yours for the taking."

"Must you toy with me at every turn? I'm an easy target, right?" she asked waving the gun back and forth.

A beautiful woman that didn't realize how attractive she was to the opposite sex was a man's worst nightmare. He'd have to fight to convince her of her own worth, and then crack skulls every time he took her out of the house to keep the blood hounds off her scent.

"I'm not kidding about the weapon. Unless you're gonna shoot me in my own house, put the gun down, Kendall."

She stared at the gun in her hand before pivoting to place it on the nightstand.

"This isn't for you."

He knew she referred to the firearm, but man, he wanted her to be all for him.

"I heard something, Cutler."

The fear he heard in her voice sobered him.

"You heard lightning split the Kapok tree next to the house. There's no one outside." Skepticism marred her features. "See for yourself," he said pointing out the window.

Branches blocked the view to outside. With the tree standing at least ten feet above the roofline, he knew it was no longer safe for Kendall to stay in the bedroom.

"Put that gun away and grab your things."

She touched the metal, but made no move to put it away.

"Kendall, what are you not telling me?"

"I'm here to fight fires, that's all you need to know."

"You brought a gun into my home, that gives me a need to know."

"The gun was in my luggage and I have a permit to conceal carry."

"Well considering you had it pointed at my chest, it wasn't in your luggage. Now, is someone after you?"

"If he is, I'll be ready."

"Who is he?"

"That's not of importance for you." She moved to bend over, and then thought better of it. "I'll grab my things when you leave."

"I don't think so." He stood with his arms

crossed over his chest. Their eyes met and held, both of them too stubborn to back down. Another flash of light cut through the darkness, before the ground rumbled beneath their feet. She jumped at the sensation. He hid his satisfied grin when her posture relaxed.

Quickly Kendall grabbed her magic bag of tricks. With the backpack thrown over her shoulder, she lifted her suitcase, holding it sideways with both hands.

"Let me help you."

"Nope...you've done enough," she shot back.

When she moved past him, her hair brushed against his arms. Oh my gosh, how had he missed the change? Layers upon layers of fiery red locks hung down her back, the tips forming a silky flame tip at the small of her back.

"Oh hell, Kendall," he sucked the air between his teeth.

"What?"

"Don't ever cover your hair again." He reached out and touched the fine hairs falling in front of her ears. His fingers tingled at the contact. Thick strands flowed through his grasp like the finest of Thai silk. "You're beautiful."

She spun around to face him, the suitcase hovering at her midsection between them—and his adrenaline-fueled focus on the storm, Kendall's safety, and the gun vanished. The real Kendall, genuine in her beauty stood before him. Where she'd been flatter-chested when he picked her up from the airport, there were rounded mounds, high and perky beneath her thin nightshirt.

"Hell's fire and brimstone, Kendall. You've gone and changed all your Mrs. Potato Head parts on me," he said running both hands through his hair. Not to mention a cool sweat had formed in his armpits from the adrenaline rush of having a woman worthy of the chase in his midst. "Where the heck did you hide those all day?" Kendall had a rack, not double D's, but more than a B cup.

She glanced down, eyeing her breasts like an inconvenience.

"They draw too much attention, so I keep them wrapped."

Cutler forced out a breath while adjusting his erection. "Kendall, women are supposed to draw attention. God designed you that way." She was packing fire in every category...body, brains, and boldness. No wonder she had to unveil herself in stages. No man could handle her all at once.

"Well, I don't want any, so I band them down."

His brain must have short-circuited because the next thing he knew the suitcase went flying and she was in his arms, fraternization rules be damned. The woman had him on fire and he wanted her blazing out of control, too.

"You have got to be the craziest woman I've ever met, Red. You can't go around springing...this and those," he said gesturing to her hair and newly discovered cleavage, "on a fella."

"See, that's why I keep everything hidden," she whispered, not taking her eyes off his lips. "You've already fallen under the redhead spell."

"You had me long before I saw your crowning glory. You want your suitcase back?"

"Should I?" she teased. "Is it my last hope to getting out of this room unscathed."

"It won't save you, darlin'."

"You never know," she said on a husky whisper. The pulse in her neck jumped and he knew she was just as effected as him.

"I'm going to kiss you, now." He brushed his thumb over her bottom lip. Her eyes never left his. "I want you to kiss me back. If that's not going to happen, then I'm going to sleep in the truck and take my chances with the storm."

"Cutler, I don't think—"

He interrupted. "Don't care what you think, right now. I care what you feel, so kiss me or help me pack a bag."

She swallowed. The tip of her tongue snaked out to wet her lower lip and he groaned aloud.

"What's it going to be, Kendall?"

She ran her fingers through his hair delighting in the glide of the soft strands. "Let's do this."

He captured her chin between his thumb and forefinger. "And afterwards?"

"Let's see if we can handle a kiss, first."

He chuckled. "I'm ready to handle you all night long," he said, claiming her mouth with his own.

Her kiss was deep and needy. He could tell she held back the edgier part of her sensuality, but he didn't know why. He pushed deep into her mouth, forcing her to open wider, to take him deeper. When she used her teeth to graze his tongue he hardened to the point of pain. When he picked her up, she wrapped those long legs around his hips, pressing her heels into the small of his back.

"Where are you taking me?" she asked breaking

the kiss.

"To our bed." He pulled back giving her an opportunity to protest. He felt the tremor in her body. She was unsure about them taking the next step, but she remained quiet.

"Nothing will happen until you want it to, understand."

"It's my choice?"

"That's right, darlin'. But I'll do everything in my power to convince you to keep your heels in the air all night."

He walked them to the futon, bending his knees as he lowered her to the softness below. He stayed atop her, settling his weight between her spread legs.

She giggled.

"What's so funny, darlin?"

"We made it longer than I thought we would locked in a house together."

"I agree with you there, but there's no going back if you let me do more than kiss you."

"Cutler, whatever happens between us tonight is over once we enter the station."

"I don't have a problem with that." When his heart started to stutter in his chest and the little voice in his head whispered liar, he ignored both.

"No drama, no hurt feelings. Those are words I live by, Cutler."

"I got it. You take care of you and I'll take care of us both. Now, if you're done laying down the ground rules, I want you naked, again."

She grinned. "You have me pinned to the mattress."

"Get comfortable 'cause you'll be here all night."

***

Kendall lifted her arms above her head. Never taking her eyes from Cutler's face. He removed her Calvin Klein top. Lust, desire, appreciation were all there in his eyes. Was she going to have sex with another man? Her husband had been her first. After the pain and rough handling on her wedding night, their sex life had only gotten worse. As a firefighter she'd grown to appreciate her schedule rotation. When her Kelly days arrived each month she dreaded the additional days at home. Why did she trust Cutler to take care of her when the man who'd promised to love and cherish her had taken pleasure in dishonoring their vows? Maybe this was another costly mistake disguised as a pleasure. She needed to protect herself...and her heart.

"Cutler...ah, do you have protection?"

"I won't leave you vulnerable, darlin'. You can trust me to take care of you."

He cupped her breasts in his calloused hands. The sensation of his heated flesh against her sensitive skin pushed her lust factor higher. He'd changed into loose gyms shorts, and he wore no shirt. How had she ever thought to resist him? She'd wanted what he had offered from the moment she laid eyes on him. Now, that he covered her with his scent, with his body, she felt overwhelmed, yet excited by what was to come.

He'd lit four candles, placing two on each side of the futon couch. Did he do that for her, or did he like to watch? She didn't care what the impetus was. The light illuminated every muscle and taut plane of his body, and she delighted in the fact that she wouldn't miss a single movement. Cutler was a magnificent physical specimen of masculine perfection. At forty, Beck was fifteen years older than her, and his body was softer where Cutler's was granite hard. He was rounded, where Cutler was chiseled.

Kendall watched as Cutler sheathed himself in a condom. She'd never seen a man do that before. The act was slow and erotic, like he was preparing himself for her. When they did this again, she'd prepare him. A sudden wave of panic washed over her. What made her think there would be a next time with Cutler?

"Darlin'?"

At his endearment for her, Kendall relaxed her lower half allowing her legs to fall open. The thought of whom her next sexual encounter would be with and when was the farthest thought from her mind when she'd left Texas. Now that she was here with Cutler, she wanted him to be her first, and her next, and the last. Light and shadow danced across his face. She glanced up into his face. His eyes were on her.

"You okay, Red?"

A playboy with a heart, yet she didn't get the feeling he was toying with her. Gosh, what had she done to deserve a man that cared enough to inquire about her state of mind with every touch?

"Yeah...I'm fine," she said clearing the frog from her throat. This act would close the door on her life with Beck, and all the painful memories she associated with this beautiful act of sharing her body with another person.

"Kendall, you're somewhere else."

She smiled. He'd caught her, but she wouldn't

pull out on her end of the bargain. "I'm fine...you can still do it, you know...since you're all suited up and everything."

Even with the low lighting, she could see his eyes had turned cold. "What do you mean, I can still do it?"

Why did he look pissed off? "I...I just meant...you can start."

Seconds later, he was off of her. The thin layer of moisture that had formed where their skin touched cooled with the air exposure. His expression now mirrored his stony eyes.

"You want me to start without you. Is that what you're saying?"

Oh gosh, he looked ready to throw her over his knee. She reached for him, but he shrank away.

"Look, Red. You're hot as fire and I want you, but I'll be damned if I'll sleep with you and you're somewhere else in your mind."

Frantic at how quickly ill-chosen words had derailed their night together, she laid a hand on his knee. "I said it all wrong. I am here with you, it's just—"

"Just what? You used to men taking your body and not noticing you're locked away in your own head space."

"Not men...one man and, yes...that's how it was with him."

Cutler's quick indrawn breath surprised her. He scanned her body from head to her bent knees and bare feet. Was he looking for some outward sign of what had been done to her? His brows were pulled low, his nostrils flared, that chiseled jawline was locked up like stone. He was angry on her behalf.

"Kendall, you're breaking my heart, darlin'. What kind of monster would want to damage a flawless beauty like you?"

Beck had stolen enough precious moments from her. Kendall would keep Cutler as long as she could. Maybe, he'd grow tired of her after one night, but it was a risk she was willing to take.

"Come here, Cutler." She held her arms open in invitation.

He pegged her with a wicked grin. "You with me this time?"

"There's no place else I'd rather be."

When he fell into her arms, she laughed, and that's when all the lights popped on in the house.

"Ugh," she screeched.

"Dang it man, that's foul," he echoed in unison.

They both looked at each other and laughed. Could she do this with the lights on? She gave the room a nervous once over. Everything seemed hidden in fantasy with the soft glow of candle light, but...now. Would he be offended if they turned off the lights, again? She was sure she could go through with the sex in the dark, or semi-darkness.

"Red."

She looked up at Cutler, their faces separated by mere inches.

"I can't have sex with you, Kendall."

Her heart sank. This was her chance to prove Beck wrong. She wasn't some cold, dry fish...not with Cutler.

"But, I can do this," she defended.

He rolled off to her side. "I know you can, darlin'," he said pulling her into his arms.

With her head settled under his chin, he pulled her flush with his body her right leg atop his, before covering them with the top sheet.

"Cutler." Did he think she was a nut job? What kind of woman took off her shirt for a man, and then went bust when it came time to do the deed?

"Yea?"

"I still want to do it with you."

His warm breath caressed the shell of her ear when he laughed. "We will, but when it's right between us."

She thought he might have been placating her, but then he palmed her right breast and softly squeezed. Her insides turned all warm and that was before he placed a string of light kisses from her cheek to her lips. His erection hardened and lengthened along Kendall's thigh. She smiled.

"I can't wait," she said closing her eyes.

***

Kendall studied Cutler as he slept. She'd awoken several times during the night to find their limbs tangled in a naked heap. She used the morning quiet to drink in every detail of his face. His messy blond waves were spread across the pillow, the first morning light giving the strands an angelic glow. With his eyes closed, she noticed his lashes were long and golden, curled at the perfect angle. She'd need to buy a $30 tube of mascara for the same effect. Her eyes dropped to his mouth. Though they hadn't made love, she'd kissed him like the John Legend song because she knew she would lose him. What had she done to warrant a man as generous and compassionate as Cutler Stevens? Not a thing.

Slowly, she bent her head until she could brush a kiss over his lips. Being this close to him her body instantly heated, demanding more than she was willing to take. Cutler had indulged her every touch, every taste last night. His eagerness to have her hands on him only fueled her cravings. As arousal bloomed in her core, she thought it best to stop kissing the hunter. When she would have backed away, a strong hand curled round her head, locking her in place. Accustomed to the feel of his flesh against hers, Kendall softened, melting into the contour of his body from chest to hip.

Blue eyes met with green.

"Morning, Red," he grinned. Dang it, he was even more gorgeous with bed head and sleep-laden eyes.

"Hey," she croaked out, not sure how he would respond to her with last night's heat a distant memory.

"Find what you're looking for?"

She squirmed beside him. "Wh...what?" Stealth Training 101 needed to be added to her repertoire. She'd been busted watching him, again.

Without warning, she found herself beneath him. "So darlin' do you like ol' Cutler enough to hang around?"

His tone was typical, playful Cutler, but his eyes were guarded. He wanted her to stay. What did she want?

"The storm ended," she managed, never imagining she would have an opportunity with a man as wonderful as this. With the weather threat gone, she didn't have a reason to be here, other than wanting to be with him.

"I know." His voice sounded raw and his hardness pulsed against the bare skin of her abdomen. Instinctively she spread her knees wider to accommodate him.

"What do you like for breakfast?" She laughed when he dropped lower to grind his erect length into her nest of curls.

"Besides that." She smiled up at his face.

He kissed her full on the mouth before turning his head to nip her earlobe. "I'll eat whatever you offer," he whispered.

When she let her knees fall near flat with the futon mattress, he gave her a long, slow gaze that lit a fuse between her legs only he could tame.

"Kendall," he groaned her name as he used his hands to caress her breasts, her belly, and her inner thighs. Wetness flooded her center. The sensation was so foreign she doubted if her ex-husband had ever excited her.

"Cutler," she whispered, reverence in each syllable. If she wasn't careful she'd fall for this man. This generous, self-directed warrior that had shown her more compassionate than the one she'd given her vows.

"Yes, beautiful." She trembled when his calloused finger stroked her petals.

"Your breakfast is ready," she breathed, her heart beating overtime. When he sucked her into his mouth, Kendall felt her carefully constructed walls quake, felt her heart opening to him. The way he touched her spoke to his skill at pleasuring a woman's body, but his caress reached deeper, satisfying a soul deep need. A moan—his, filled the space, driving both their pleasure closer to the brink. Cutler had a big appetite, and she recklessly spread her legs wider giving him a bigger big plate.

By noon, they had eaten a chicken spinach quiche she'd prepared, kissed enough to set a new world record, and eventually drove into historic Key

West for errands. She thought he would've taken everything she offered, but he'd teased her with only a taste of what he could do with that mouth. Her body burned like a hungry succubus deprived of a long awaited lover. When Cutler pulled to a stop in front of the community center in Bahama Village, Kendall's urge to mate vanished as a knot began to form in her stomach.

"I promised to drop off the baseballs and bats for the kids. Come inside with me," he said grabbing her hand.

"No, I can't."

A profound sense of dread and loss swamped her. A reminder that last night should have been the end of it between them again came to mind. She'd crossed a bridge too far with Cutler this morning. Now, he expected a woman she could not be for him.

He laughed until he noticed she hadn't moved.

"Red, come on." He nudged her. "The kids would love to meet you."

To hide the pain churning inside, she snapped at him. "I said no." She pushed his hand away.

"Okay. You want to tell me why you won't come inside?" he asked, his jaw tight. Confusion marred his handsome features. "I usually stay an hour or two, but I'll come right back."

"No, and... I don't want to hold you back." She spoke the truth. Cutler deserved a woman less impulsive and more giving than she was capable of. "We passed a novelty shop on Whitehead. I'll walk up there while you hang with the kids."

"You can take the truck, Red."

That made her smile. "Thanks, but I could use the walk."

The furrow between his brows had her leaning over to plant a kiss on his lips. "Have fun and come back safe," she added.

That broad smile she'd fallen for overnight spread across his lips.

"They're pre-teens, not the Dallas Cowboys defensive line," he chuckled, exiting the truck with her.

Sixty minutes later she crossed the final block to find Cutler leaning against the truck's tailgate.

He smiled when he spotted her.

"I just finished up. Want to do an early dinner in town?"

"No, I'll pass on dinner out."

His eyes dropped to the white plastic bag in her hand. "You pick up something red and racy for tonight?"

Oh, he thought she had lingerie in the bag.

"This is a gift...for you." She blushed when she recalled the message she'd selected for the front and back of the t-shirt. She knew Cutler was wrong for a woman like her, but she wanted him to remember their night together.

Kendall opened the bag and pulled free the peace offering.

Cutler read it aloud, "She loves blonds."

He burst out laughing, his bass echoing in the empty lot.

"There's more on the back."

He wiped at his eyes. "By all means, show me darlin'."

Kendall laughed too when his eyes watered.

"But, I prefer redheads."

He swept her up in her arms. "I love it, Kendall...thank you."

She acquiesced when he claimed her mouth with a deep, slow caress of his tongue, licking his way inside until she moaned his name.

"Anywhere else we need to go before heading home?"

Gosh, he made it sound as if this was their

everyday routine. She had to stop this before he got hurt.

"Cutler, do you mind if we head back to your place now?"

He took her hand in his before she could finish her sentence.

"I need to grab my things," she paused, "before you drop me at the hotel."

He pivoted to face her, his face a readable collage of surprise, confusion, and hurt.

"Yeah, Red. I do mind."

His body stood ridged, ready for the challenge. Okay, her clean break was going be messy.

Chapter Six

The Monday morning sun beat down on Engine No. 10, making Cutler race against the clock to remove the soapsuds before they streaked the finish. Snow white clouds hung overhead erasing the last vestiges of Friday night's storm. Kendall had stayed hidden from him since he dropped her off at her hotel on Sunday night. He knew she was in the firehouse because several of the guys had commented on the Texas redhead. Those silky ribbons had covered his chest when he'd used his body to cradle her head.

He finished the wash and dry job in under an hour with Trace and Nathan's help.

"Ladder looks good, Cut." Nathan rounded the rear end, bucket of water in hand.

"Yep. Thanks for the help."

"Would have gone quicker if you were focused on the job rather than scoping the station every ten seconds for Kendall."

Trace was all about business. The guy didn't spare women a second glance. He barely had time for his two best friends.

The door to the Captain's office opened and Kendall stepped out with the boss at her back. Cutler moved towards her before he thought better of his actions.

Kendall kept her eyes on the Captain, even when he moved closer to her. Why the heck had she been avoiding him? When she still hadn't acknowledged his presence and his boss stared at him like get the freak out of here, Cutler lost it.

"Kendall, can I talk to you for a moment?" he snapped. Could he get more middle school, boy meets girl?

"Stevens," she finally turned to look at him. "Let me finish with the Captain and I'll come find you." As though a robot had replaced her, her eyes were a muted green, flat and dull. What happened to the woman who'd kissed him every chance she got and made him breakfast? Was the T-shirt supposed to be a consolation prize? Well, she could have it back because he wanted her instead.

"Sure thing. I'll be waiting." By the time he reached Nathan and Trace at the truck, they both stared at him with expectant looks. He ignored them, instead choosing to watch Kendall.

The standard issue uniform fit her like a suit of

armor. Armor that had all her gorgeous hair pinned up, breasts strapped down, and emotions buried. He hated the look. Hated that she felt the need to hide who she really was.

Nathan blew out a breath, his gray eyes cautious. "Cut, maybe it's best if she got away."

"Why is that?" he asked, his tone sharp.

His friend ran a large hand through his midnight strands before he spoke.

"We didn't meet during my trip to Dallas, but I heard talk of Kendall. She's a good firefighter, but prefers handling things on her own. A few times a month, the crew volunteers with the city youth league. Kendall flat out refused to help with the youth league. The team considered her a loner."

Kendall had enjoyed Cutler's company. She made the choice to stay with him last night, but what kind of public servant declined a few hours of their time to toss a ball with kids?

"She's the one I want," Cutler said, his eyes on Kendall. He didn't say the rest of the thought. She's the one he wanted to keep.

Kendall was headed in their direction when the bell sounded. Everyone in the station began to move all at once. The vibration of the alarm signaling he was needed somewhere in the city never failed to get his adrenaline pumping.

**

Kendall spied the determined look on Cutler's face across the firehouse bay. His golden mane was tame today, brushing against his uniform collar in neat waves. She liked it better mussed from her fingers. The gorgeous firefighter had occupied her thoughts even after he'd dropped her at the La Koncha on Saturday. She sensed he wanted an explanation about her sudden withdrawal. How could she tell him he deserved a woman better than her—someone less tainted? Kendall's phone chimed an incoming message. The sight of Beck's number on her phone pitched her gut into a nauseating spiral. She should have deleted his contact information. She opened the dialogue box. Reading the message, she had to throw out a hand to steady herself on shaky legs.

You lying witch. The doctor's office called about where to forward your birth control pills. You'll wish you had pushed out my baby. See you soon, wife.

He'd discovered her secret. She should have

known the fight for her freedom would continue, but...she had hoped...

"Raine, you're with us," Cutler called out.

"I'm ready, Stevens." She'd avoided the firefighters all day, refusing to let Cutler get her alone, but the strength to fight him fled in light of the text message. All her reserves were needed for when Beck arrived. And he would come, she just didn't know how he would try to manipulate the Captain into giving him what he wanted.

How could Gordon's office have made a mistake of this magnitude? Sally was meticulous in her record keeping. Kendall had all her prescriptions delivered to the DF&R fire station. In making that phone call, the clinical staff had violated her privacy and opened a door to hell Kendall had thought closed. Beck would kill her now that he knew she'd conned him into a divorce. When Beck arrived, he'd find her armed for battle.

***

The acrid smell of charred wood and scorched earth greeted Kendall as Engine 10 pulled to a stop at the scene on College Avenue. Blue skies that normally surrounded Stock Island, which lay a mere two miles northeast of Key West, were alight with red flames. Their engine was the first on the fire scene. Nathan's experience in command and control was apparent, as he'd located the facility's address and divided the building into quadrants. The location of the address served as the alpha side, with quadrants assigned in a clockwise fashion. Acting as the crew's Fire Captain, he was already on the radio.

"Dispatch, this is Engine 10. We have visible smoke and fire at the Charlie-Delta corner on the fourth floor of a four-story structure. We're assuming instant command, fire attack. I'll do a three sixty, and then supply an update," Nathan said ending the call.

Considering a four-story building was a high-rise structure, Kendall knew after Nathan's jog around the perimeter he would be calling for additional engines and trucks. Law enforcement would be needed for traffic control and directing occupants, staff, and visitors.

Billows of gray clouds, thick and dense, hung like a goth backdrop around the remains of the Island Life Senior's Village.

Kendall jumped from the rig. "Oh my gosh." Her grandmother's best friend, Mrs. Elliot, had an apartment in the village.

The fire raged near the back of the building, but most of the damage appeared to be concentrated on the top floor.

"Station 3's ladder truck ETA in two minutes," Matt, their engineer called from behind the wheel. Generally a four man crew consisted of a firefighter, a fire medic, who served as both a firefighter and a paramedic, a driver engineer, and a crew captain. Kendall was an extra fighter onboard. With their engine being the first on the scene, Matt would be responsible for supplies, working the water pump, and cutting the building's utilities until the ladder truck crew arrived.

"Has everyone made it out?" she asked.

Kendall couldn't wait. Her grandmother had friends in residence. Matt had oriented her to the compartments and equipment on the engine upon arrival that morning. With the last of her turnout gear secured, she grabbed her self-contained breathing apparatus, or SCBA.

Cutler appeared at her side. "Trace and Nathan will take the two and half line to the charlie-delta quadrant." He called out over the residents and facility staff gathered in the parking lot. "You ready?"

"Do you ask the guys the same question?" Instead of waiting for him to answer, she yelled to the staff member huddled over an elderly gentleman with an oxygen tank. "Miss, please move him and all the residents across the street. Do you have the names of every resident out here?"

"No, but I can get that information," a woman said.

"Law enforcement will be on the scene ASAP and will request the information."

Kendall started coughing, just as Nathan seemed to appear from the pillar of flames. He must have been able to circle the building. That would be great news for the engine assigned to confine the fire exposure to the additional structure. Someone grabbed Kendall's wrist. She looked down, the woman she'd directed to corral the residents away from the engine and the building regarded her with tear-filled eyes. "Mrs. Elliott is missing."

Kendall's lungs froze. Her Grandma Dinah visited Mrs. Elliott every week. She would be devastated if anything happened to her knitting buddy. "Is she mobile?"

The young nurse nodded her head. "Yes."

"Where would she be in the building?" With a fix

on where the retired attorney should be, Kendall would save time on searching the structure.

"Her room is on the third floor."

"I'm on it." Her grandmother would never lose another person she loved to a fire.

With her fire axe in hand and a Haligan tool on her utility belt Kendall sprinted for the doorway she spied leading into the building. A building this size would have one stairwell in each corner. Usually, two would be designated for evacuation and the remaining for fire attack and equipment. Cutler would catch up to her. Grateful for a well-conditioned body, she took the stairs two at a time. Physical fitness was one of the many things Beck had insisted upon. He also made her keep her devil-red hair covered, her sinful breasts bound, and her mouth closed. Thanks to rigorous workout routines, the seventy-five pounds of gear she'd donned felt like a second skin.

Rounding the corner, she ran into a man dressed in scrubs with a wet towel draped over his head, a sooty scarf contrasted with his dark skin. She motioned him forward.

"I'm fine," he said, "but I can't reach the rooms on the third and fourth floors. Four is under renovation and we were in the process of relocating the residents to the lower floors."

"You go on now. I'll search the building." She moved to place her air pack on his face, but he refused.

"No, I'll make it. Help the residents as best you can."

"The hose should be behind me. Stay low and follow it out and away from the building."

When Kendall reached the third floor, she was body slammed by an elderly woman. The petite woman held a dry cloth over her mouth and nose. Kendall grabbed her just as her eyes rolled to the back of her head. Cautiously Kendall lifted the limp body over her right shoulder. Why hadn't Cutler caught up with her?

Sweat coated her from head to toe beneath her gear. She could taste the smoke in her throat. Ignoring the discomfort in her lungs she hefted the unconscious woman higher on her shoulder.

Rounding the corner to the second floor, Kendall stumbled into Cutler carrying the black man in the scrubs who'd waved her onward.

Even through his shield, she could see the tight set of his jaw. "You left him. You left me."

"No, he was ambulatory when we passed each other."

"You left before the assignments were complete. Did you direct him to one of the evacuation stairwells?"

Oh God, she hadn't. How could she have been so foolish? In her haste to reach Mrs. Elliott, she'd placed another victim in further peril.

When she opened her mouth to explain, he turned and walked away.

Paramedics swarmed them the second they exited the building. Kendall lowered the woman to the ground. Her back protested the low crouch. Paramedics took over, an oxygen mask was placed over Mrs. Elliot's face while another member on the team assessed her vital signs. With the oxygen displacing the toxic air from the fire, the patient began to cough, deep and ragged. Thank goodness. Her grandmother's friend should recover, but she still needed to be checked out at the hospital.

Two ladder trucks, each at opposite ends of the building were in place. Soon crews would be on the roof ventilating the space. Once the smoke and heat were evacuated, the fire attack crew could progress with better visibility and conditions to extinguish the flames.

The female staff member that had realized Mrs. Elliott was missing ran over.

"Thank you, thank you. You're my hero."

"You're welcome," Kendall responded out of courtesy. She didn't feel like a hero, quite the opposite.

Kendall turned to rejoin the crew. When a hand landed on her shoulder, she turned anticipating one of the staff members.

It was the Captain.

"Kendall, you're back in the engine."

She turned to her crew, but none would meet her eyes. She took in the Captain's grim expression. Kendall nodded her head in understanding. Her decision to leave the man to exit the building on his own had been a bad one. The decision to enter a burning structure without her partner could have been deadly. As she walked back to the engine, she replayed her decision to leave Cutler behind, to continue up the stairway when the staff member needed her help. Even thousands of miles away from Dallas and Beck, her impulse to act alone without considering the cost still plagued her.

Chapter Seven

Kendall slammed the door to the women's sleeping quarters. Inhaling deep, she sank down against the door and let her lids drift closed. The tension of what had happened on the scene held her body captive. Muscles felt knotted and tight from her neck to her lower back.

Torturous was a good word to describe the engine ride back to the station. Nathan and Trace kept their eyes straight ahead, pretending to ignore the charged air between her and Cutler. His ice-blue eyes bore into hers the moment he'd climbed into the engine after her. Why had she run into that burning building without backup? Before pivoting and running toward the crumbling structure, she'd seen Cutler's expression. It was riddled with disbelief, fear, and anger, but she couldn't focus on him. She had to show him, show them all that she didn't need any help. Other women needed heroes, not her. Kendall saved lives, including her own. She was a good firefighter, just as capable as a man.

The doorknob turned. She jumped away from the

door at her back, afraid he would force his way inside.

"Kendall, unlock the door."

She didn't need him ranting at her; she had extensive background knowledge on dragging herself over hot coals.

"We can talk tomorrow. Please leave, Cutler." She prayed Captain Brady would let her finish the two-week assignment.

"Not till you explain to me what the heck you were thinking storming into that building, alone."

"We got everyone out, didn't we?" she challenged.

A heavy thud sounded against the door and her heart skipped a beat. "I could have lost you." His voice softened.

Her heart sped up. Cutler's words penetrated her tortured soul, providing comfort.

"We could have lost you out there or the guy on the stairs."

With a sigh, she shoved his truth from her mind. Rubbing her eyes she hoped the gesture would erase how close she'd come to jeopardizing the very people she'd sworn to protect.

"The rule is two in, two out."

She knew the rules. Knew she'd placed the crew at risk...placed Cutler at risk. "I know," she whispered.

"Then why?" came a solemn voice through the door.

The room was all of a sudden too small. Cutting off her air supply. Shame and disgust at her actions flooded her gut. She felt exposed and vulnerable in a station filled with ten of the people that should be able to trust her judgment. Would the guys ask that she be removed from the rotation? If they did, Kendall alone was to blame. *Why had she taken the risk?*

Kendall had to face the crew sometime. It might as well start with Cutler. She twisted the lock and pulled the squeaky hinges wide.

Warm ocean breeze filled her nose. Then Cutler, messy blond locks and steel-cut jaw, came into view. He wore the same uniform from earlier, traces of sweat and debris stained the fabric. She eyed his expansive chest, recalled the feel of his taut muscles beneath her fingertips.

"I can do this," she whispered, referring to the job and the man before her.

Worry had replaced Cutler's icy stare from

earlier. She pushed out a breath in relief. Maybe, she wouldn't have to fight with him. The man had seduced her with one look, and won her heart with a good meal and dessert that started with him stroking his tongue into her mouth. Fighting was the last thing she wanted to do with him.

He stepped inside, closed the door, and then locked them in. "You said those exact same words to me our first night together. Who are you trying to prove wrong, Kendall?"

The sexual need building in the deepest part of her came to a halt. An image of Beck, smug and towering over her prostrate body collided with her fragile defenses.

Fear, raw and cutting caused her knees to quake. God, he would come for her. And just like before, Kendall would be powerless against his influence. She stumbled back, slinked down the wall, letting the weight of what was to come drag her down to the cool tile. When her butt hit the floor, she let her head fall forward. Her hands formed a bowl for the tears that fell.

"Kendall?"

She wiped at her damp face. "You can't save me, Cutler."

He dropped down to his haunches in front of her. "Ah, darlin'...don't go challenging a Marine by telling him what he can't do."

Kendall balked when his strong arms came under her knees and behind her back.

"Stop fighting me. I don't want you to get hurt."

Not his demand, but rather his concern for her, put the breaks on her thrashing. He grunted and stilled. Had she hit some vital part of his anatomy?

Turning her head away from his chest, she looked up. Gazing back at her, all vestiges of humor gone, was Cutler the warrior. She could imagine him in camouflage, his weapon locked and loaded. His eyes shone bright with a possessive protectiveness and... Kendall wasn't afraid. He must have recognized the change in her.

"That's my girl."

When he lowered his head to take her mouth, she was already out of the starting gate, pressing eager lips to his.

She inhaled him, pulling images of their entwined bodies forward. Her brain then her body synced with his, and she relished the connection on more than a physical level. He was right. Kendall was so...his...girl.

***

Cutler felt his heart stop when Kendall ran into that unstable structure. Though they'd just met three days ago, he felt a thread of connection between them. Whatever emotion or whomever had drove her into the flames needed to be excised before she left on another callout. Surprised that the female sleeping quarters mirrored the men's layout exactly, but on a smaller scale, he carried her into the bathroom.

"Shower first, and then we eat."

Grateful that she didn't argue, he placed her on the counter top, and then crossed the room to one of the glass stalls and turned on the water dial. Kendall remained where he'd placed her.

When she made no attempt to look at him, he tried to goad her. "I could come closer. I remember how my scent gets you irritable and naked."

She stared up at him.

"I messed up, Cutler."

He could hear the *again* she didn't say.

Cutler hated to see the devastation in her eyes. Her shoulders shook and tears started to flow down her cheeks again.

"Donnie, the guy with the scrubs is fine. He called to check on you. Guess he'd never seen a real female firefighter. You're an instant celebrity."

She shrugged. "If that is true, tell the Captain to prepare for a tabloid scandal." She spread her arms wide, "I can see the headline, Key West's First Female Firefighter Risks Life of Crew and Victims because she can't let go of the past," she trailed off.

Cutler blew out a breath of frustration. So, she'd been preoccupied with thoughts of her former lover.

"So, you want him back?" A surge of jealousy spiked like a rogue charge in Doctor Frankenstein's lab.

She startled as if he'd struck her.

"Never. I never want to see Beck again. I was referring to...never mind."

Cutler's breath eased once more. He had been prepared to put in the horizontal, vertical, and diagonal hours necessary to make her forget the man she'd left in Texas.

The hiss of hot water hitting cool tile reminded him the station had a limited supply of hot water.

Stepping between her spread legs, he dropped a kiss to her nose.

"In the shower with you before the guys use all

the hot water."

She reached up and pulled the tie from her hair. Ribbons of red silk cascaded down her back. "Into the shower with us."

Cutler froze. Long fiery lashes swept lower, and then opened, revealing emerald eyes smoldering with lust. Lush lips parted, her pink tongue extended as she completed a slow journey of invitation across the bottom one for his viewing pleasure. He swallowed...hard.

"Kendall...if we start,"

She stopped his next words with a kiss to his mouth and a palm to his erection. The nip surprised him, but then he remembered their first in his living room. The pent up energy he'd felt roaring through Kendall's limbs as he pleasured her. He let her taste him, sucking her deeper with every tongue stroke. Sensing her satisfaction with his response, he resisted the urge to pull her back to him when the kiss ended.

"I won't stop you."

He leaned in close. "Remember those words later tonight."

Cutler lifted her off the counter. He turned her to face the mirror.

"Watch me," he commanded.

Slowly, he unbuttoned her uniform top, one button at a time.

He frowned when the ACE bandage securing her breasts came into view.

"Lift your arms," he growled.

Kendall did as she was told. Moments later her full breasts, ripe and tanned sprang free.

He fixed her with a hard stare. "You're with me now. No more hiding your body, Kendall."

ACE wrap gone, he filled both hands with her tender globes, rolling the nipples between his thumb and forefinger. When she groaned, he licked a moist trail up the side of her neck before he captured her earlobe between his teeth. She shivered. "You're beautiful, darlin'."

"I'm glad you think so."

"I know so, Kendall. You're a beautiful woman."

With a hand to her back, he applied pressure till she leaned forward.

"Stay where I put you." Efficient hands had her pants pooled around those long legs in seconds. Cutler groaned aloud when he saw the skimpy red lace covering her toned backside. "Red's my new favorite color," he teased as he dropped to his haunches.

"Oh," she said, wiggling her hips, "I had hopes you'd like creamy white and petal pink, too."

An image of her core, moist and wet slammed into him in 3-D. "Oh heck, I got myself a nasty girl."

"Dirty talk a problem, cowboy?" she asked teasingly.

"Darlin', that's my first language."

Cutler kissed and nibbled down her legs, applying long strokes to her smooth flesh. He took delight in the fine tremors that racked her body at his touch. Her breaths came in rapid and rough spurts. Would she sound the same when she orgasmed for him? His hand hit hard metal and he froze.

"Red." He hesitated. "You carrying?" If Kendall had a weapon on her at all times, what kind of danger was she expecting, and how much time did they have before it came knocking at the door?

"It's...not the gun, just pepper spray."

He gazed up. Her eyes were fixed on the mirror.

"I didn't want the guys to notice, that's why it's strapped to my ankle."

He moved to stand, but she hit him with a weapon guaranteed to stop him in his tracks.

"I'm wet." She inhaled a deep breath then said, "And I want you inside of me."

She spread her legs wider. The scent of her arousal reached Cutler's nose, and he gripped her hips to steady himself. Slowly he lowered those sling shot panties, until bare flesh, sweet and fragrant greeted him. Gently he opened her, touching the core of her femininity, sliding through her moist folds. His fingers came away with slick cream.

"Cutler, I want..."

"So do I," he said. Reaching into his wallet, he made short work of shedding his clothes and donning a condom before he turned her around to face him.

Cupping her chin in his right palm, he angled her face up to meet his. "Let me know what you like, darlin'."

The easy smile she gave him, transformed into a hitched breath, and then a groan when he surged forward burying himself deep inside her welcoming flesh. Her back arched and he pulled her down harder onto his erection. Oh man, Kendall was so tight his toes dang near curled under the soles of his feet.

"Red," he hissed. Her muscles milked his shaft like a velvet glove. Never had a woman gripped his mind, body, and soul so completely. "Work me over, Kendall."

Cutler was helpless to control himself. He pounded into her, pushing her head closer and closer to the glass lining the wall. Damn, it was like he was trying to carve out a shelf for himself inside her.

"Please, Cutler. I need more," she panted.

He nodded, cupping her face in his hands. He kissed her, the press of his lips against hers hungry and bruising. She was breathless, her chest heaving when he stopped.

In a voice husky with lust, he said, "Turn around and face the mirror."

Cutler lifted one of her knees onto the counter, opening her core fully to him. He drove into her body. He continued to thrust when she gasped. Her fist clenched tight around the faucet as she sought to hold on for a long ride.

"Is this how you want it?" he growled at her ear.

"Yes," she moaned.

Sweat glistened on her nude back. He leaned over her, snaking his tongue up her spine.

"Nice touch," she tossed over her shoulder, lids at half-mast, breathing ragged.

"Ah darlin', my touch is going to be all you remember about today." Hell, he'd already forgotten his name, rank, and serial number. The controlled charm he was known for...gone. He took a deep breath, pulling Kendall's scent deeper into his lungs. The urge to claim and to mark intensified when she pushed back meeting his thrusts.

"You want more?"

"I can handle you," was her response.

He cursed because if she took him any deeper he'd be screaming her name.

Slowly he withdrew, panting with the effort it took to leave her body.

"No," she whimpered, as she reached back to dig her nails into his ass.

His voice came out as a raspy bellow, echoing in the tiled space. "I like that you marked me, Red." He spun her around to face him. Cupping her buttocks he said, "Lock your legs around my waist."

The moment her legs circled his waist, Cutler drove up into her moist, wet heat again. Slick friction as her body accepted his invasion was nearly his undoing. She strained against his erection, spreading her legs wide to accommodate him.

He entered the shower. Kendall tossed her head back, letting the water shower down her fiery locks, darkening them to a rich crimson. When her back made contact with the cooler tile wall, she hissed. Her internal muscles quaked before tightening on his erection.

"Hold onto me," he commanded.

At the feel of her arms tightening around his neck, Cutler's vision tunneled. He saw only her. He caged her with his arms, his elbows pressed to the wall above her shoulders. He felt as if he were fused with her. Their grunts and moans mixed with the rain shower crashing down on them. Her plump toasted nipples were hard as her breasts bounced up and down with each thrust and retreat. He hissed when her nails clawed his back.

Mine, mine, mine ran in cadence through his head. He gripped the back of her head in one hand. Pushing his fingers into her hair, he pulled her head up. Their eyes met.

"I'm gonna come, Red," he panted, pounding deeper, anchoring her hips in place to take him full force. "Come with me."

Her mouth opened, but he heard no sound. Then he felt the ripples of her sex, pulling at him, sucking him deeper into her velvet soft center. Every inch of his body clenched, and then exploded. His eyes rolled back in his head. A roar ripped from his lips as his release jettisoned from his body. Concerned he'd left her behind, he nearly collapsed to his knees with satisfaction when she screamed. Pulsing, rhythmic waves stroked the length of his hardness. Her eyes flashed a kaleidoscope of emerald green as she orgasmed.

She groaned before her head fell forward and she buried her face in his chest. The course sound was bliss to his ears. Using his weight he pinned her in place.

Cutler cupped her face between his hands. "You good?"

She nodded, the effort to speak would deplete precious energy reserves. He'd felt reborn inside of Kendall. All the charming facade that he wore for other women stripped away. Never had a woman satisfied him so completely. When a cloud of darkness settled in her eyes, he about shattered inside.

"What's wrong, Red? Did I hurt you?" Was she having regrets? He didn't believe she'd acted impulsively, but could he have lead her to where he wanted them to go? His chest constricted.

"No," she whispered, "you didn't."

He relaxed a fraction. "Kendall," he paused, "I don't care about your past. You hear me? You feel perfect in my arms, Red. We fit," he breathed, "we...fit."

"Cutler." Her green eyes burned with emotion that he recognized as fear. "Don't love me so good that I can't let you go when it's time."

He tightened his hold on her, not wanting to lose the connection so soon after their lovemaking. His heart pummeled in his chest, defenseless against this courageous woman who'd cracked his soul open and chained herself inside. He felt his manhood swell with need.

"Too late, Red." He lowered his mouth to hers. "I can't stop now," he said as he drove into her again.

She scored his back with her nails.

"Cutler," she heaved. "I can't orgasm again."

He grinned. "You'll have to prove it, darlin'."

Minutes later she exploded around him, sucking him into another sweat drenching orgasm.

"You proved me a liar, Marine," she teased. He released his grip on her thighs, lowering her until her feet touched the cool tiles.

"Oh, don't be hard on yourself. I'm gifted." He smiled, pleased that his woman was happy. "I think I'm putting you to bed before round three."

She gave him a sultry smile. "Maybe you should.

The water is getting cool."

"What my lady wants, she gets." They bathed in a flash and without delay he exited the shower and carried Kendall to the bed. He smirked in satisfaction as she yawned.

"Get some rest. I'll wake you when the food comes." He smiled when Kendall snuggled under the blanket and closed her eyes.

"Thanks, Cutler." He was about to correct her when a knock sounded at the door. There would be no, *thank you* quid pro quo between them. She was his.

In his bare feet, Cutler pulled on his pants before slipping his wrinkled T-shirt over his head.

It was Trace at the door with two bowls of pasta.

"She okay?"

Though his brain knew Trace had no romantic interest in Kendall, it wrangled Cutler that his friend seemed to have a connection with her. Call him cocky, but he didn't like other men asking about his chick. "Yep, we're talking it out."

Trace's nostrils flared, and then he narrowed his eyes at Cutler's state of undress. "You talk before or after sex?"

"Gimme the dang pasta and stay the hell away

from this door unless I text you, man."

Trace shoved the two bowls at him. "She gonna stay or leave?"

"Kendall's not going anywhere." Whatever fueled this reckless need for her to prove she was worthy of a position she was more than competent to hold, they would deal with it one day at a time...with her in Key West.

Chapter Eight

Kendall stood in front of her locker, surveying her sleeping quarters. Thank goodness she was the only woman to use the space. The room scented of her, Cutler's warm ocean scent, and lots of sex. A twisted heap of bed sheets had been pushed to the foot of the bed, more evidence of Cutler's physical prowess with her body.

A tap, tap, tap rapped on the door.

"Kendall, we have a situation. Could you join me in my office?" Captain Brady said from the hall outside of her room.

Kendall's sex hungry brain instantly sharpened. Her body was still warm and satiated from the hours of loving Cutler had plowed her with during the night. Too limp to move when he dressed to leave at o'dark thirty, she had rolled back over for another hour of shut eye.

Having the Captain summon her personally couldn't be good for her continuing at the station.

Ignoring the churning in her gut, Kendall grabbed her uniform shirt from her locker. Her breast ace wrap lay on the top shelf. She smiled. Though Cutler hated the thought of her binding her breasts, he'd left the choice to continue wearing the thing up to her.

During her marriage to Beck, she'd had no choices. She considered the possibilities. With Cutler she had affection, support, and passion all for the asking. Lifting the ACE band, she ran her forefinger over the ribbed pattern. A relationship with Cutler would be different. Her heart flipped and tripped over itself. Her fresh start could include Cutler.

Raised voices beyond the door had her jumping. The door handle rattled. She finished dressing and ran a hand through her flattened waves.

"Hold your hoses. I'm coming." She grinned donning her boots. If the Captain thought she'd rush to get her walking papers, he didn't know women.

"Kendall Aisles, I don't like to be kept waiting."

The air left her body. Beck stood on the other side of the door. Pounding began between her ears. What had he said to the Captain? Her lungs refused to inhale a full breath. Instead, a mixture of choppy exhales followed by equally choppy inhales kept her from passing out. She checked her boot. The Mace can was in easy reach.

With a firm hand, Kendall turned the knob. Beck and Captain both wore a grim expression, but for different reasons. Her ex-husband looked the same. His dark brown hair with gray at the temples was combed back off his broad forehead. His tan skin bore fine lines around his deep set, dark eyes and his thin lips were pressed into a hairline fracture of disapproval.

Captain Brady cleared his throat. "Kendall, it seems your husband…"

She and Beck interrupted simultaneously.

"Ex-husband," she stated, matter-of-factly. Of course, he spoke over her.

"You can call me Chief Aisles." Beck gave the Captain a cordial smile.

There was the southern Baptist charm that had roped her in after he'd attended her parent's funeral. She'd lapped up his ever-present support and direction like a needy child. With her grandmother in a care facility recovering from a heart attack, she'd felt so alone. Beck had been her savior.

"After all I was Chief of Police before I put a ring on Kendall's finger."

He raked his eyes from her boots to her curls that hung loose around her shoulders. Cutler had stroked her tresses all night and she had to admit, feeling the length of the thick tresses between her shoulder blades reminded her of their night together. When Beck's eyes narrowed on her breasts, Kendall had to fight the urge to cross her arms over her chest. As his irises darkened to black, the subtle signs of pent up rage registered on his face.

"My, my, a few months away from home and you forget yourself, Kendall."

She lifted her chin hiding the fear skirting down her spine. What would he try if he got her alone? And what would she have to do to stop him?

"My home is now Key West." Why had she blurted that out? Her paycheck still had Dallas Fire & Rescue on the payee line. She and Cutler hadn't discussed her sticking around after two weeks.

"Captain Brady, you have to excuse my wife. She's been under a lot of stress on account of her having problems conceiving like a normal woman."

Kendall closed her eyes in equal parts rage and embarrassment that Beck, once again, had brought their drama to her job.

"Maybe, it was your mature sperm with their crooked back stroke," she jabbed, forgetting her boss stood between them. Three years of marriage to Beck came flooding back. The snide remarks and subtle put-downs had started before they left for their honeymoon. Instead of her husband being honored by his wife's virginity, Beck had told her she was a lousy lay, storming out of their wedding suite and leaving her alone. Well, he wasn't worth the ink on diary pages, either. Their mental sparing had eventually evolved into physical blows.

A crimson-faced Captain interjected, "Okay you two. Raine you're still on the clock for now. Get to work."

When Beck shook his head no. Brady hit him with a lethal stare. "This is my station, Chief Aisles. Seeing as your visit is of a personal nature..."

"Red."

Kendall's eyes shot wide open at Cutler's voice. His long legs were covering the bay separating the men's sleeping quarters from hers.

Beck turned his back to her and the Captain to address Cutler.

"I'd appreciate you addressing my wife by her proper title, boy."

"Well, damn," the Captain muttered under his breath. "Cutler, I'm handling this," her new boss said as he stepped forward.

"Yea, Cutler. Pretty boy like yourself," Beck jibbed, "I'm sure you can find another man's woman to sniff around."

Cutler took a step forward, a sly grin on his handsome face. "I think I'll keep sniffing around the one I got."

Beck stiffened unused to being challenged. Then she saw the change in his demeanor and knew he was about to hurl a curve ball. Kendall stood immobile, not sure how to keep this train on the track.

"Well now, Kendall, it looks like you got yourself a Captain America type," Beck chuckled. "Think he'll still want you after I press charges for assault and conspiracy to harm an officer of the law?"

"What are you talking about?" Cutler asked.

The Captain regarded her. A sinking feeling dropped in her belly. Good heavens, between the fire and this daytime soap opera drama, she should start reviewing online job postings today.

"This is not the time or place for domestic disputes." The Captain looked squarely at her.

At least their marriage squabbles at DF&R happened without her boss in a front row seat. With her humiliation complete, Kendall took a step toward Beck, ready to throw him out of the firehouse.

Cutler snagged her wrist. His hold tight, but not bruising.

"Don't worry, Captain. Nobody in this dispute is domesticated." Cutler's words held more warning than reassurance.

"You're right about that, boy. Kendall's a little reckless. Aren't you, wife?" Beck laughed, the sound harsh.

Her skin tightened, the cells in her body stilled because she knew what he'd say next.

"I've always liked that about her until she hired a couple of thugs to rough me up." Beck turned cold eyes in her direction. "I guess it's the native spirit in her. I miss our sparring, suga'."

Cutler stared at her, his face unreadable.

"You paid—"

Cutler stopped short when she all but nailed his male anatomy to the wall with her eyes.

A smirk covered Beck's haggard face. "Yep, my lovely wife is a true public servant. Finding novel ways to employ the underbelly of society."

Kendall held her head high. Cutler had to know she would have never taken such drastic actions if Beck had threatened her after he nearly killed her. After she tried to move out of their house, he'd found her. One visit from Chief Aisles and she needed an emergency room and a cast on her left forearm. Gordon had recognized her from one of the many social events she attended that first year of their marriage. He offered to help her, but she'd turned him down the first time. She was thankful for his persistence.

Cutler looked away from her, meeting Beck's arrogant smile.

"Kendall may have been your wife in the past, but I can promise you, bubba, she's mine now."

To prove his point, he snagged her around the waist, hauling her up close to his body. Oh, he was still in her corner.

"Go get your things, Red. Our shift is over and I'm taking you home."

Beck reached for her, but Cutler was quicker at stepping in front of her.

"If you touch my woman, fire and rescue won't be able to save your sorry ass," Cutler growled.

Well, today was off to an interesting start.

Chapter Nine

Cutler entered Hobo Alley, tossing his keys on the highboy tabletop. Thank the stars that Happy Hour started at seven o'clock in the morning in Key West. He didn't look over when Kendall pulled out a stool and took the seat next to him.

"You paid a thug to beat up your husband, the chief of police?" Cutler struggled to wrap his brain around the implications of Kendall's actions. What else didn't he know about this woman? The woman he'd shared a bed with for hours. A blazing torch of vindication backlit her emerald gaze.

"I took plenty of ass whippings for free, Cutler. A broken arm can be a powerful tipping point," she snapped. "What's the problem?"

He couldn't believe what she was saying. "You could have asked for help, Kendall. Gone to the police."

She turned narrowed eyes on him. "You mean the cops that worked for Beck? The ones that saw the bruises on me and looked the other way? Or how about the patrols that came by because the neighbors heard us fighting? Is that the help you're referring to?"

"Look..."

"No, you look. I don't need you judging me and I sure don't need your permission to protect myself." She stood to leave. He grabbed her wrist.

"Please...don't leave. I'm sorry. My brother, Lance is a sheriff in Marathon. I can call him —"

"It's fine," Kendall interrupted. "I can take care of myself. I didn't come to Key West to complicate my life or yours. Let's just end things now," she sighed.

No response to the last part of her statement. "You should have told me, Red."

"Cutler the reason I didn't tell you about Beck—."

He interrupted. "Is the same reason you don't have to tell me now."

She sat back down. He felt confident she would stay, so he loosened his hold.

"I never imagined things would go this far between us."

"Your redhead spell is a good one," he teased, trying to lighten the mood.

"I spent three years in a marriage with a cruel man. Please don't talk down to me."

"I'm not," he said, meeting her eyes.

She ran slender fingers through her hair. Her frown telling him the last thing she wanted to do was talk about her marriage.

"A friend of mine, Gordon, is a doctor. He placed me on birth control pills."

"Lots of married women decide when to have children."

"Not without telling their husbands."

Cutler grinned. "You tricked your husband into thinking you were infertile?"

She nodded. "Yes. It was the only way he would release me from the marriage. So, if you're going to keep up with the snide remarks or judgment, I can walk back to my hotel."

"Don't think so, darlin'. I'm pissed that you kept the fact that you had a crazy ex-husband playing Smoky and the Bandit with you, but I'll get over it."

"So what are you saying?"

Kendall came wrapped in complications with a big, fat 'I did some crazy shit to get away from my ex-husband' bow, but he couldn't leave her now. He doubted he ever could.

"I'm saying you stay with me. I'll handle Chief Aisles when it comes time."

"Rachel," Cutler called out, "Gimme two

breakfast platters and one Dogfish IPA."

"Seriously, a beer at this time in the morning."

"Well, I'm not interested in the Kool-Aid your ex-husband was serving up back at the station."

"Hi Kendall," Rachel said as she sauntered over from behind the bar. "Whatcha' having to drink with your breakfast?"

"Can I get a hot tea?"

"Oh honey...I've got beer, wine, liquor, orange, tomato, and pineapple juices, and Coke products."

Cutler watched, but he kept quiet. He liked that she didn't feel the need to fill every moment with conversation.

"Bring me the pineapple juice and a glass of water."

Kendall tried to smile when Rachel stood there, appraising them both. She could have saved herself the energy; Rachel seemed to know what made her customers tick from the moment she met them. Hobo Alley held its own sort of magic because of Rachel.

"Cut, what's wrong?"

Rachel was right to ask. Cutler's usual easy smile and laid back demeanor was clearly absent.

"Kendall's ex-husband, Chief of Police Beckham Aisles, is in town 'cause he wants her back. Seems the good ole' boy doesn't take to kindly to losing something he considers his."

Cutler knew men who treated women like objects to be bought and sold. He understood how Beck's mind worked. Her ex-husband probably never valued her, rather he had a need to possess beautiful things. Her deception had sparked his need to control and punish. Beck wanted Kendall to suffer for bringing their marriage to an end on her own terms.

Thin arms circled Kendall's shoulders. "Don't you worry, honey. We take care of our own. Ole' Beck will find it real hard to get anywhere near you," Rachel said, confidence infusing her words.

Cutler said nothing, letting Rachel's words settle over the table like the promise it was. He could count on his friends to have his back.

Kendall's lips parted in surprise. She looked at him trying to understand what was happening. He told her the truth.

"You're mine."

She stared at him, beautiful and proud in her challenge.

"That's it? Do I get anything else?"

"What more do you need, Kendall? I'm a simple man."

Their food arrived. Flapjacks, two strips of thick-cut bacon, a sausage patty, and three scrambled eggs covered the platter. Cutler picked up his fork and went to work. He looked over to see Kendall hadn't touched her plate.

"Eat up, Red. I have plans for us." He wiggled his brows in suggestion.

She gave him a weak smile. A deep furrow had taken up residence between her brows.

"Beck won't go away. You don't know him like I do. He'll make trouble for both of us."

Did she doubt his ability to protect her? Cutler would fight to keep her. The Marine in him wouldn't have it any other way.

He managed to keep his voice low as more of the regular customers began to fill the tables around them.

"You don't have to worry about Beck anymore. You're not alone, Kendall."

Conversations from nearby tables floated by, but their table could have doubled as a prayer altar. If Kendall said a word, only God could hear it. The rusty protest of the front door opening drew his attention. Both Nathan and Trace had changed out of their uniforms and were headed in their direction. Claudia, the hot guy table server, let loose a throaty version of a police siren.

"Hey fellas, what can I get ya'?"

"The special," they replied in unison.

Kendall sat tense, not meeting anyone's eye. Last night when he'd gone to check on her in the women's sleeping quarters he'd had every intention of explaining that the guys didn't blame her for what had happened with the man in the stairwell. When she'd opened the door he could tell whatever had upset her was far more disturbing than what happened at the scene. After he'd taken her into the bathroom, all bets were off and he'd found a new purpose for his visit.

Nathan, the diplomat in the bunch, tackled the uncomfortable silence. "I can't stay long. Adam's out at the house keeping Symphony company."

Symphony was expected to deliver their baby any day now, and Nathan didn't like leaving her alone. Adam, or Gandolph the Gray to the Hobo Alley frequenters, had been Symphony's neighbor in the trailer park where she'd lived before her marriage to Nathan. The old timer loved that woman better than the father Symphony never knew and guarded her like a pit bull.

Nathan directed his comment to Kendall. "Glad to know you're going to be staying around."

Her head shot up. She swallowed hard, but there was no hiding her grin. "So, you guys are still good with me on the team?"

Trace cut in. "Why wouldn't we be?"

"I just thought after yesterday...maybe, you wouldn't—,"

"Look Red," he jumped in. "None of us are perfect. My heart stops every time we roll up to a scene and there are people still inside or someone's lost everything they own because of a fire. I can't imagine what it's like to have a loved one trapped in a burning building."

All three men nodded their agreement. Cutler's gut did an about face and a quarter turn when tears sprang to his woman's eyes.

"Besides," Trace said, "your ex-husband is a human booger with a badge. When he walks into a room, you feel like you've touched something nasty."

They all burst out laughing. Kendall's phone ringing cut through the laughter.

Cutler began eating his food when she took the call.

When she noticed him watching her, she

mouthed. "It's my grandmother."

"Tell her you're in good hands," he whispered. When she turned beet red, he instantly hardened. It was time for them to get Kendall home...and back to bed.

The color leeched from her face.

"Red, what's wrong?"

The conversation at the table stopped. Nathan and Trace looked at her expectantly.

"Beck called," she said, her voice trembling. "He's on his way to my grandmother's house."

Hell's fire and damnation. "Can I speak to her?" Cutler asked, not sure if Kendall was ready for her grandmother to know about him. When she hesitated, he reached for her. Taking Kendall into his arms, he held her close, and then he spoke in a tone for her ears only. "I want to help, Red. I promise not to hurt you or your family."

She bit her lip. "Beck is dangerous. I won't let him hurt her." She handed him her phone, and Cutler couldn't help but notice the sure intent in Kendall's eyes. How far would she go to keep her freedom from her ex-husband? A better question was how far would he go to help her?

"Mrs. Dinah, this is Cutler Stevens," he said.

When he would've continued with his plans of how to fix this situation, she started with a barrage of questions.

He stuttered as he began to sort and choose which questions to answer, cause there were a lot. "Yes, ma'am...no I don't think highly of Chief Aisles. That's true."

Kendall reached for the phone, but he shrugged her off. No way would he mess up this job interview. If Grandma wanted to make sure he was fit to be a part of her granddaughter's life, he'd was ready to ace the test.

"Yep, I really like her...well, that's up to her. I...I hope so, too. Yes, I like conch fritters. Okay, we'll meet you at the Sands Outlet on US Highway 1. We're leaving now."

He disconnected the call, handing the phone back to Kendall.

"What's happening?"

"You grandmother is coming to stay with us."

"Us?"

"Yep, you're moving in with me. Tree cutters took care of the Kapok and the roof is fine." He took her hand and strode towards the exit. "We need to get on the road. Beck has a head start."

Cutler didn't like anyone getting the jump on him. It wouldn't happen again.

***

Her Grandmother Dinah was settled in Cutler's bedroom. She still wore her silver hair in one single plait down her back. Though her granny stood barely above four feet, she had a bold personality. A trait Kendall wished she'd adopted earlier in life. Later that evening, Cutler wore a brown t-shirt with loose lounge pants, his IPA bottle in hand. The double size mattress on the futon lay open, an invitation she found hard to resist. By the gleam of mischief in Cutler's baby blues, he'd done the deed on purpose. As much as Kendall hated not joining him on the futon, she'd feel like a 'bad girl' if she slept with Cutler knowing her granny could hear them from the other room.

"You want to kiss me…goodnight?" she asked.

Oh, that was code language for please drag me back to your cave and sex me silly.

"Darlin', I plan to kiss you all night, but you gotta come closer and stop stalling."

She'd wiped down the kitchen until it sparkled

with the Good Housekeeping seal.

"I just came out to say goodnight."

Cutler's mouth gaped open. Kendall had hoped to avoid having this discussion. No such luck.

"You plan to sleep in there, not with me?"

She threw up her hands. "It's my grandma, Cutler, not a girlfriend. I can't have sex with the granny cam on."

"It's not a secret we're sleeping together. Your grandmother knows. Heck, if my granny was alive, she'd know too."

That was his argument? She waited, hoping he'd say more, but nope, nada, the well had run dry.

"How would it look? I'm recently divorced. I got here four days ago, and already I'm in your bed."

"It was a bad marriage. So what if you slept with me on the first or the hundredth day. We'd still be together."

Cutler sounded so sure about them. She preferred to think in the present. Her future and their longevity was in too much of a smoke haze to be clear on anything beyond the here and now.

He took a slow pull off his beer bottle. Kendall sighed as the liquid clung to his lips.

"She'll be asleep soon enough. Then I'll hook you

up," he teased.

Heat, moist and creeping spread up her neck and down her thigh. Cutler hadn't taken his eyes off her, the blue irises fringed with ice cool flame. How had he known that she wanted him, craved him? She needed to change the subject before she jumped his bones right here and now.

He grinned. "We can do that too. Let me eat something, and then we can disappear in the laundry room for a quickie."

Her mouth dropped open. "You reading minds again?"

"Nope, but I'm a master at female body language." He leaned in close. His breath tickled her right ear. "You're squirming in your pants, darlin'. And," his voice dropped an octave, "without your breast sling, I can see your nipples ridged beneath your shirt."

She gasped.

"I know you're wet, Red."

"Hey my grandmother is in the other room."

"Yeah, well, she'd better stay there or she's about to witness one for the record books."

Two hours later a sexually satisfied Kendall slid into bed next to her prone grandmother. She'd joined

Cutler in the shower afterwards, hence the second hour.

"He seems like a nice young man."

Her grandmother's voice emerging from the darkness startled Kendall.

Kendall shook her head, amused by her response. "Grandma," she sighed. "I'm sorry if I woke you."

"You didn't, dear. I don't sleep well away from my bed." There was a pregnant pause, so Kendall held her breath praying her grandmother would let the conversation drop.

"I can see he's quite taken with you."

"You just met him today, how can you be so sure?" Even she had her doubts that Cutler would keep her around for the long haul.

"I have eyes, Kendall. The man is smitten with you. Plus, I heard how much you like him, several times in fact, about an hour ago."

Kendall's breath hitched. "Grandma, I thought you turned your hearing aids down at night."

Her grandmother chuckled. "Not when there's a hot guy close by."

Kendall rolled over and clicked on the bedside lamp.

Her grandmother's face held a mischievous grin. "He smells good, too. Like the beach in spring time, a sweet freshness with a salty chaser...yum."

"Grandma, I think you might be a little freaky."

"Don't say that down at the senior citizens center. I could barely keep them from stealing my thongs when I lived there."

Kendall covered her ears. "I can't hear anymore."

"Me either after all that ruckus I heard about an hour ago." She blushed. Being close to Cutler she forgot how to be quiet. Admittedly, it was nice to get out of her own head. One touch of those thick, callused hands swept her troubles under the bed, at least for a few hours.

"Sorry, grandma. We won't be here very long."

A warm hand, gentle and soft, settled atop of hers on the sheet.

"You can stay, Kendall."

She sat up straighter in the bed. "What?"

"With your parents gone and that horrible marriage over, you don't have to leave," she began. "You're alone there, I'm alone here, but...now you have Cutler and me...." Her grandmother trailed off.

Kendall wasn't sure what lay between her and Cutler. She couldn't go changing her life based on a few days, could she?

"Grandmother." She hesitated. How did she tell the matriarch of the family that she was just sexing her co-worker, nothing more?

Her grandmother must have sensed her uneasiness because she patted her hand and then rolled over, her back to Kendall.

"I'm happy that you're here. I won't be staying with you and your man friend. I'll spend a few days at the hotel, so I can visit with Mrs. Elliott. All the seniors have been moved temporarily in the housing tower on Sigsbee Road. It'll be a two mile commute, instead of eighty."

Kendall was happy her grandmother had a friend. Lucky for them she thought. Where would Kendall be once this thing with Cutler was over?

Chapter Ten

Cutler ground his molars together. The winds blew off the Atlantic filling his truck with the fresh morning air of spring. The sun filtered through Kendall's flowing strands, giving them an internal glow. He craved her with an intensity his words and body struggled to communicate, but something was off. Kendall had been ignoring her cell phone calls for more than a week. Interesting, he noticed if the call was from Beck she told him, but when it was from Gordon she either ignored it or clammed up.

"Who's on the phone, Red?"

Kendall had become increasingly tense each day the phone calls persisted. What reason did she have for avoiding talking with anyone? He knew about the marriage. He understood and accepted the actions she'd taken to gain her freedom.

"A friend from home."

She didn't meet his eyes when she spoke.

"So, it's Gordon," he growled. Why wouldn't she come clean with the entire truth of what happened back in Cockrell?

"Yeah, it was him."

"Why aren't you taking his calls?" Had she been sleeping with Gordon once the marriage to Beck went south? He sensed she was still running.

"Because of you," she answered.

He tilted his head from the road to look at her. Her expression was closed, and he didn't want to make her life more difficult.

"What's going on between you and him?"

She rolled her eyes. "Cutler, I'm here with you. There's nothing going on with me and another man."

"Darlin', when my mother wasn't rolling my old man for money or making him believe she was his one and only, she was cheating on him. You don't have to get physical to wound someone, Kendall."

Her tan complexion, paled. "You think I'm cheating on you?"

Cutler knew he was projecting his childhood issues onto Kendall, but he couldn't 'unthink' the thought.

"The reason why I never stayed with a woman for long before you was because either, I was gone or she'd be gone before things could go sour. It's different between you and me, Kendall. I want you to stay, but you're hiding something and I don't like it."

Her expression looked like she carried a truckload of concrete on her back. "Cutler," she paused.

Eyes, normally vibrant green, looked worried as they landed on the leather seats, the center console, everywhere but his face.

"Gordon thinks there may be something between us."

He shot flaming arrows across the small cab. "Another larger than life Texan to contend with, Kendall? Are there any other men you need to tell me about?"

Kendall flinched.

He reined in his frustration when she scooted closer to the passenger door. It wasn't her fault she was a woman that men found attractive. He trusted her, but her unconventional methods of handling conflict left him on edge.

"He's been there for me. I thought...I thought, maybe we would be good together."

"So, it was your idea. You've been leading him on?" Cutler roared.

"No," she stammered.

His blood heated to a boil. So, she was playing him. Using Cutler to get rid of her ex-husband so she could go back to the doctor after her two weeks were up.

"You're lying, Kendall."

She turned toward him, tears in her eyes. "I'm not lying. I told Gordon I might be interested in him."

She jumped when Cutler banged his hand on the steering wheel.

"I trusted you," he ground out.

"And nothing has changed, Cutler. I promise you. Gordon and I talked about us before I met you."

"Then why are you avoiding his calls?"

A grimace formed on her beautiful face. Dear God, Kendall had manipulated him and probably... Had he been wrong to put his faith in her?

"I feel guilty for inviting his interest. I knew there was no passion between us, but he made me feel safe."

"That's all there is to it?" he questioned, feeling his blood pressure drop to below two hundred.

"He's been kind to me...I don't want to hurt him."

Doubt again crept into his mind.

"And the pills were all about getting away from Beck, nothing else? You want children, someday?"

Kendall's brows furrowed. "Cutler, what are you

asking? Beck wanted children. I could never bring a life into a marriage like ours. He threatened that he would divorce me, take everything if I didn't conceive. So, right or wrong, I created the conditions to make the threat a reality. Beck didn't think I could be alone after my parents died." She hadn't either...at first. "In the end, my freedom was all I wanted. Now do you understand? I can't hurt Gordon after all he's done for me."

He'd hadn't known about her parents. A woman, grieving the sudden loss of her family could explain how she'd married a guy like Beck. The revelation was yet another example of why the secrets she harbored had to end.

"So, you'd rather keep me in the dark?" Cutler left out the fact that she'd ripped a hole in his chest by not trusting him with the truth. Why couldn't she accept help?

They drove the rest of the way home in silence.

"Cutler, please try and understand what it was like for me. I had no one. I need to figure out how to let him down."

In other words, she didn't want or need his input. "Seems like you figured that out real fast with me," he muttered.

The hiss that filled the air sucked the oxygen out of the front seat.

He growled in frustration, but he held his tongue. In his peripheral vision, he saw her reach for him, then stop shy of actually touching his skin.

"I'll call him when we get to your house."

He didn't care for her tone. It was monochromatic and flat, the opposite of Kendall.

"Red, I...I want to listen when you talk with him." What if this guy was another obsessive type?

"Why? Because you want to control me or you don't trust me to end things with Gordon?"

Her accusation grated. "No." He forced himself to stay calm. "I don't trust him or any other non-related man when it comes to you. You're mine."

When he pulled the truck up in front of the house and cut the engine, Kendall didn't make a move to get out of the cab.

"Red?"

She shook her head like an insect had landed on her and she wanted it gone.

Angling her body sideways in the passenger seat she faced him, verdant eyes swirling with emotion.

"When I took this assignment, I told myself two things. One, rebuild the relationship with my

Grandma Dinah. I've been a terrible grandchild, infrequent calls, even less frequent visits, but my granny loves me just the same."

Cutler thought he might love Kendall, too.

She smiled, but it didn't reach her eyes.

"The second thing was, I'd focus on the damage done to my career at the hands of my ex-husband."

"Those are all worthy goals." Where was she going with this?

"I told myself..." She swallowed, "No men."

Anxiety gripped his breath. Kendall was the one for him. He'd waited for the 'but you changed all that for me', never imagining the woman meant for him would walk into his life. Kendall didn't say another word. Now that he had her, he couldn't lose her.

Cutler reacted without considering the impact of his actions. Threading both his hands through her hair, he wrapped the strands around his knuckles and tugged until he looked into her upturned face.

"I'm not letting you go, Kendall. You're it for me."

He felt the shudder in her body, saw the light dim in her eyes.

"You know, you sound so much like Beck, it's breaking my heart."

The words hit him in the chest like the blunt end of a Haligan tool.

"Kendall, I didn't mean it like that. I'm sorry if—"

She pulled away from him, eyes hardened with determination, that chin of hers jutted forward like a suit of armor.

"I think I'll go hang with my grandmother at the senior's center."

Though her eyes never left his, the light behind that earthy green had dimmed. In an attempt to avoid being hurt, he'd wounded her. Not sure how to repair the damage, he blurted out the first words that came to mind.

"I'm sorry, Red, but don't leave before we can talk this thing out. This whole other man thing is making me a little crazy."

Kendall looked aghast at his comment. Damn it, he was making it worse. He knew she was an innocent, her husband had been her first lover and he'd basically accused her of being a whore. Before Cutler could regroup, she had the door open and was climbing down from the cab.

"I'll be back to get my things."

The last thing Cutler heard was the door slam. What had he done? More importantly, how would he get the woman that held his heart back home...permanently?

***

Kendall refused to let the tears fall. The moment her grandmother's yellow Mustang convertible pulled onto Roosevelt Boulevard headed south, Kendall started packing up her memories of Cutler to seal away in one of those all-purpose, vacuum seal bags. Dinah watched the road with her left eye and Kendall with the right. A parade of scooters and premium collection rental cars whizzed by them. Her grandmother didn't seem to notice; used to the tourist congestion on the roadways. As they drew closer to the senior center, Kendall's heartbeat grew a little quieter. As she had done so many times in the past, she dug deep into her core strength and found...she'd hit the bottom. Dear heaven, she felt the walls start to shake. Cracks opened, geysers shot from her foundation, she was falling apart. She loved Cutler, but now it was over. She had fooled herself into believing he could accept her once he knew the truth.

"Kendall." Her grandmother's voice was gentle.

"Ma'am." It felt good not to be alone, but she wanted...no, she chided herself. It would not have worked with Cutler in the long-term. Did she want forever?

"Why are you leaving him when it's obvious you don't want to?"

She drew in a shuddered breath, determined to get the words out.

"We...he..." Say it she demanded of the heartbroken woman threatening to leap from her chest and run back home...to Cutler. "Cutler needs something I can't give him."

Her grandmother clucked her tongue. "Nonsense. You're a Raine. You descend from generations of competent and capable women. Women who celebrated their womanhood, rather than try to hide it. Women who valued a man strong enough to admit when he's wrong."

Kendall lowered her head, not wanting to reveal her thoughts. Maybe the competent and capable gene had skipped a few generations. "Cutler doesn't trust me, Grandma."

They reached the designated visitor's lot for the senior center. When her grandmother cut the engine, she didn't exit the car. Kendall looked down at the last remaining member of her family. Grateful that she would have this connection when she left in three days.

All at once, her grandmother appeared to have aged twenty-years, her skin shallow and drawn. "Are you okay?" Kendall asked.

"Yes, I was thinking about what you said."

Kendall twisted in her seat to retrieve the picnic basket loaded with fresh baked mango bread, raspberry scones, and apple danish for Mrs. Elliott.

A two-story apartment building housed the seniors until the village could be rebuilt. The cause of the fire was still under investigation, but arson was suspected. The first floor held a cafeteria and an activity room that led to a rear courtyard. A cluster of three smaller structures designated for administrators, therapists, and maintenance flanked the palmed oasis forming a perfect square. The staff and visitors used a network of porticos to transit the grounds.

"Don't bother yourself with my drama, I'll figure it out."

Her grandmother raised her head, dark brown eyes seasoned with wisdom regarded her.

"Will you figure out that you demand trust you

are incapable of giving? Her grandmother's head tipped up, the long braid, draped in front of her shoulder. "These decisions to isolate yourself leave you vulnerable. You're choosing to put yourself *at risk* again."

Kendall's grip fell slack around the handle. The word again punched her in the gut. How many times would she have to hear that word, from herself and others?

"That's not true."

"When your parents died—"

Kendall held up both hands, palms facing Dinah. "I don't want to talk about them."

"Because your mother—"

"It was another one of Mom's ideas for them to volunteer their time," Kendall hurled the accusation. "She couldn't get herself out of the youth center when it caught fire, so Dad..." Kendall's voice cracked. "So Dad had to try and save her."

Small hands gripped her shoulders, shaking her.

"Your father made a choice to save the woman he loved." Gone was Dinah's gentle tone. This voice was coated in steel.

"But, he failed," Kendall sobbed. She'd lost both her parents that day.

"No, Kendall, he didn't. He got those kids, himself, and your mom out of that building."

Kendall dried her eyes. "They died due to their injuries. I don't want help that puts other people at risk. I can take care of myself."

Her grandmother released her. "You refuse any offer of assistance, Kendall." The look she gave bore pity. "From your family and friends, and certainly on the job."

"Grandma, how can you say that?"

"Because, I'm too old to lie to myself about who you really are. You never trusted me to help you when you ran into trouble with your marriage. Cutler loves you. You love him, yet you don't trust him enough to tell the man what you need or how he can help you."

Tears spilled down cheeks lined with age, a lifetime of love, and concern. "Think of the fear and how helpless your parents must have felt knowing they would never see you again. The pain I live with knowing my only grandchild won't confide in me or come home when she feels lost in this world."

Kendall's defenses crumbled. How had she hurt the people she cared about most, when she only sought to protect them? Her impulsiveness had led to so many poor decisions, she wanted to shield...not isolate them.

Her grandmother took the basket from her hands.

"Maybe it's you who can't accept the woman in the mirror, not Cutler. Mrs. Elliott is waiting. Come inside when you're ready." Dinah slammed the door, leaving Kendall alone with her guilt and shame.

Was she ready to come in out of the rain? Could she allow the people that cared about her to help?

Preoccupied with the husband who'd failed her and the authorities that never came to her rescue, Kendall hadn't considered how she'd hurt her grandmother and Cutler by not sharing her feelings and refusing their help. In her selfish quest for self-reliance, she had proven her lack of faith in them both. She wanted to be like the Raine women before her, capable and competent, in every aspect of her life because...she loved Cutler. Her heart beat faster at the admission. The crazy man was direct and confident and...he wanted her, unconditionally. She could be fearless and declare to him how she felt. Was it too late to for her to make amends?

Kendall reached Mrs. Elliott's apartment, her backpack over one shoulder. The floral wreath on the door obscured the unit number. Knocking, she waited as her thoughts settled on Cutler's face when she'd gotten out of his truck. Raised voices on the other side of the door grabbed her attention.

"You stay away from me. What have you done with my friend?"

That was her grandmother's voice. Kendall tried the knob. The door opened just in time for her to see Dinah head-butt a woman approximately Kendall's same height with bright red hair. Seconds later, her grandmother crumpled to the tiled floor.

"Grandma," Kendall screamed as she rushed forward.

The other woman stumbled, but quickly regained her balance. It was then Kendall noticed the syringe in the redhead's hand. When she would have charged the attacker, the barrel of a gun stopped her.

"Kendall."

She didn't know anyone in town except for her squad and the folks at Hobo Alley. Who...Kendall's brain screamed as she changed the hair color to blonde and added fifteen pounds to the frame.

"No," she breathed. "It can't be."

"Glad you decided to visit today. It saves me the phone call to tell you Dinah suffered a freak accident while checking in on her friend.

"Sally?" Gordon's nurse from Cockrell was here, in Key West, with an eerie Kendall Raine makeover. "What are you doing here?"

"I came to claim what should have been mine."

"Sally, there's nothing going on between me and Dr. Stein." Had the woman been secretly in love with the good doctor all along?

Sally smiled wide, a schoolgirl grin on her too thin face. "Don't be silly, Kendall. I came for Beck."

Bells and whistles sounded in Kendall's brain. Sally had seen the physical abuse she'd suffered at the hands of Beck. How could she possibly...

Sally aimed the gun at Kendall's chest.

"You won't take him from me, again."

Dear God, Sally was insane. The reality of Kendall's situation was more savage than a horror story. A wolf in sheep's clothing had fallen for a wolf hiding behind a badge and...they both were after her.

***

Cutler suspected when he telephoned Nathan, that his two best friends would come to his aid. Dinah had arrived within minutes to collect Kendall and her luggage. With him on chauffeur duty it had kept her close to his side. Had she viewed his need to be near her differently? The accusation that he was behaving like her ex-husband had him downing his second longneck in twenty minutes. The chatter at their hot guys table was non-existent. Rachel and the rest of the Hobo Alley regulars watched him like a bunch of pigeons perched on a power line.

"What happened, Cut?" Nathan didn't make eye contact when he asked the question. Of course, Trace looked him straight in the eye.

"Kendall moved back into her hotel suite."

Trace set his beer bottle back on the scuffed tabletop. "You upset?"

"Heck yeah, man," Cutler barked. "She accused me of treating her like that asshat, Aisles."

Both men jerked.

"Whoa, Cut. That's a low blow." Nathan shook his head before ordering a longneck.

Cutler nodded in agreement.

Trace, who generally could be counted on for at least two words during a conversation shocked them both. "Are you?"

"Am I what...acting like her abusive ex-husband? No." His response was emphatic, but his gut knotted that his friend had to ask.

Cutler was out of here. No way would he sit here while his friend compared him to Beck. He stood, prepared to drive over to La Koncha and have it out with Kendall.

A heavy hand to his shoulder pulled him to a halt. "Sit down, Cutler."

What was Trace's problem today?

"You wanna get your hand off me." The rush of an impending fight coursed through Cutler's veins. His fists clenched at his sides.

Nathan grabbed his wrist. "Don't, we're here to help."

Cutler jerked away from his friends. The Marine in him ready to do battle against anyone who thought he would hurt Kendall.

"Eleven days," came Trace's deep rumble.

"What are you blabbering about?" Man, who knew that Trace could actually talk too much.

"Kendall's been on staff for eleven days and she hasn't been out of your sight in that time. You work, live, and sleep together. When does she get some breathing room?"

Dear sweet baby in a manger, Cutler never considered he'd smothered Kendall with his affection. Man, how had he been so blind? Had he lost her with his need to control their time? He wouldn't let himself believe they were over.

"Maybe it's best if Kendall returns to DF&R at the end of the week."

Nathan's statement yanked him from his stupor.

"Wrong answer." No way would he open himself up to that conversation. He and Kendall had a good thing going. The bed buddies were always available, but the forever kinda woman...that was Kendall.

"It's getting complicated, Cutler...especially with the ex-husband hanging around, huh? You like your relationships on the dry side of the fire hydrant. No two guys in a pissing contest, remember?"

What kind of help was Nathan offering because he sucked butt at couples' counseling.

Cutler gritted his teeth. "Kendall and I are not complicated. She's with me. That's where she'll stay." He hoped Kendall was her own woman. Imposing his will on her would only push her farther away.

Nathan and Trace regarded one another, a slow smile covering both of their ugly mugs.

"Glad to hear it, Cut...because her husband asked Chief Brady to send her back to Dallas today."

"Not that asshat, again." Before he could go off on a rant, Rachel called out to him from behind the bar.

"Cutler, the firehouse is on the line."

He'd left his phone in the truck. Had Kendall tried to reach him, too? He strode to the bar, taking the cordless phone from the barkeeper's hands.

"Cutler, here." It was an administrative staff member on the other end of the receiver. Why would anyone who knew him telephone the station?

"A Dr. Gordon Stein keeps calling the station for Kendall. We've tried her cell phone, but she's not picking up. You want me to patch him through?" the woman asked, her tone polished with professionalism.

"Yeah." Might as well size up my competition.

Beck picked the wrong day to come storming into Hobo Alley. Cutler spotted the arrogant son-of-a-gun long before he found his target. The other scanned the faces in the thin crowd before locking eyes with him.

"Where the hell are you hiding my wife?" Red faced, Beck's gut moved faster than his legs as he crossed the floor to stand before him.

"Ex-wife," several of the patrons called back.

Dressed in a white button up with black stitching around the pocket and black jeans, Beck glared up at him.

"Boy, you have no idea what Kendall is capable of. You think you can handle her. Trust me she needs a strong hand to keep her in line."

Cutler narrowed his eyes on the poor excuse for a human being. "Keep her name out of your mouth."

Ignoring the Chief as he started to sputter, Cutler zeroed in on the good doctor's refined voice when the call connected. The man sounded frantic. Cutler heard the name, Nurse Sally, job reference in Key West, and disturbing memos left behind in her desk. As it became clear what the doctor was relaying to him, the bottom dropped out of his stomach. He hung up the phone.

"Cutler?"

He heard Rachel's voice, but he didn't respond. Beck's arms were flailing and jowls jiggled at being ignored. Every cell in him vibrated, the long ago sensation of raw fear awakened, but not from a stranger's M-16 or an IED beneath his feet, no...this guttural response emanated from his heart. His brave and courageous woman, who'd applied her intelligence and skill to orchestrate an escape from a marriage that threatened to crush her untamed spirit, needed him to stand beside her...to fight for her.

"Nathan, Trace," Cutler said, processing what he needed to do. "Kendall's in trouble." Nathan was right. Being with Kendall would take him back to a place he'd left behind. Guns, bullets, and killing didn't belong in his present, but Kendall did. He realized in that moment that the lies, the secrets held no weight. Kendall was a fighter, a survivor, and he would do anything to keep her safe...even if it meant burying a bullet deep in anyone that threatened her.

When he pushed past Beck, the man foolishly grabbed his arm, delaying him from reaching Kendall.

"Hey, don't walk away from me boy. Kendall's my wife, if she's gotten herself into—."

Cutler spun on his heel, using his bulk as he advanced, forcing Beck to crane his neck back and up to met his eyes.

"Say my woman's your wife one more time and your ass is alligator bait, you feel me, man?"

He headed for the exit, leaving the asshat speechless, with Trace and Nathan on his heels.

***

Cutler barreled a diagonal line across the Kmart

parking lot taking a back road to the senior citizens' property. He retold Gordon's story to Nathan and Trace, his white-knuckled grip tightening on the truck's steering wheel. He had to make it in time. Regardless of the danger, he would save Kendall and convince the stubborn woman to stay by his side. His heart depended on it.

"You know Beck is following us, right?

Cutler glanced past Trace's shoulder out the rear window. "Yeah. Man, I'll deal with him after I get my woman safe in my arms."

"Heck, Cut." Nathan grinned. "You're in love."

"Probably," he said, whipping the Chevy into the first available spot beside the residential building. The realization not scaring him half as bad as the thought of losing Kendall.

Cutler leaped to the ground. "I'm going after—" the blood stilled in his veins. Panic raced like a runaway locomotive through his gut. By the look on Nathan and Trace's faces they smelled it too. Smoke.

Kendall was a good firefighter. She would have called it in, made sure everyone had exited the building, unless.... Had she been rendered helpless?

Within seconds all three men entered the rear courtyard, via a side portico. The structure closest to the residents was ablaze. The flames an intense blue, told him this was not the source of the smoke he smelled from the parking lot.

Trace reacted first. "Cutler, go find Kendall. I'll assess the scene, while Nate call's this in to the station. You have three minutes."

With a plan in place, Cutler took off at a run.

***

Kendall sniffed the air. She wished the burnt stench of popcorn filling her nose equaled a bad movie night, but the acid churn in her gut told her different. A fire roared nearby. The first tickle of smoke reached her airway triggering a cough. Sally stood in the combo living-dining room, a glass table and taupe couch at her back. The four-foot window had a metal cross weave insert to keep the residents safe. No way, could they escape the second floor there. Kendall could subdue the woman on her own, but would she have enough time to get her still unconscious grandmother to safety? They were in Mrs. Elliott's one bedroom apartment, but Kendall couldn't be sure of the other elderly woman's whereabouts. From her position by the door, the galley kitchen to her left was empty. Along the same wall, the door leading to the bedroom suite was ajar. Maybe, Mrs. Elliott was in there, drugged and helpless. God, she would need help to get both seniors safely outside. With the fire distracting the staff and residents, no one would come to her aid. Cutler's easy smile, crooked and wicked, came unbidden to her. He would help, if he knew she were in danger. For the first time since her parent's death, Kendall knew she could depend on someone other than herself and...she loved Cutler.

Kendall's cell phone rang in her backpack. She ignored it. Not now, Gordon.

"Sally, I smell smoke. We should get my grandmother and Mrs. Elliott to safety." Kendall hoped her plea would appeal to the caring nurse that had helped her months earlier.

"I know." She beamed like a child with her favorite ice cream on a hot July afternoon. "The first fire was a test. This time it'll look like an accident."

"Please, Sally..." Kendall had to try to reach her.

"You ruined him, Kendall. It was supposed to be my turn after Beck got rid of you. I exposed your lies, but instead, he came here for you. You left me no choice. You'll die so Beck and I can be together."

"I don't want him, so you don't have to hurt anyone." Kendall's phone buzzed again.

Sally's smile faded and her hand tightened on the gun handle. "He wants you." Her lips began to tremble. "So you see? If you're alive, he'll still want you."

Vibrations and chiming came from her backpack. Gordon must know that Sally is a threat. Once again, Kendall realized he had been trying to help her and she had refused his aid by not answering the phone. If she got out of this, she would not make the same mistakes.

Her grandmother's slumped form began to stir behind Sally. A part of her wanted to rush forward, but impulse could lead to tragedy. Her gun and the Mace were added hazards in this instance. Fire and bullets, limited air supply and Mace were deadly combinations. Tendrils of smoke curled from the bedroom door, but Kendall felt heat creeping up her back. There were multiple concealed fires...in a medical environment. If the fire reached an oxygen tank, the building could blow.

"Who keeps calling you?" Sally screamed before a coughing fit cut the sound abruptly.

"It's Dr. Stein." Kendall remembered to apply her

limited psych knowledge choosing to refer to Gordon by his formal title. Sally's fixation seemed to solely focus on Beck, but Kendall could use an advantage.

"Another one of your admirers," Sally shrieked. Rage twisted her once lovely features into a macabre mask.

In the hallway, Kendall heard raised voices above the crackle of burning wood. Moments later a male voice rose above the chaos in the room.

"Kendall, where are you, darlin'?"

Hope soared in her heart at the sound of Cutler's voice.

"Wreath on the door," she yelled above the hair splitting pop from the bedroom. The fire could double in size in less than thirty seconds. Time worked against them with every second that passed.

Footfalls grew louder until Cutler pushed through the door, stopping short of slamming into her back. He gripped both her arms, swinging her behind him in one fluid move.

"Thought you could use some help, Red."

Kendall would've responded, but then Beck entered the room. Used to being in charge, he stepped in front of Cutler, a physical intermediary between them and Sally. Kendall watched as Sally's eyes lit up.

"Beck, you came." Sally lowered the gun and crossed to go to him, but then…it all went wrong.

"You alright, Kendall?" Beck kept his eyes on Sally as he addressed her. "Kendall, suga'?"

This was Beck, the lawman before her, the one that had cared for her during her darkest hours. Maybe, he'd loved the wounded woman that she was following the funeral. In reality, once Kendall learned to cope with the loss of her parents, her true personality had reemerged. Beck hadn't liked her independent spirit and she didn't need his heavy-handed oversight. They were gasoline and fire, an explosive union…with each one potentiating the other.

"I've got Kendall," Cutler replied backing her out the door with his bulk. He gripped her wrist tight, yet she felt the gentle stroke of his thumb over her pulse point, like he needed to reassure himself she was real. Her heart swelled with more love for him. How was that possible?

Peering around his tense muscles, Kendall sucked in a breath. Sally had stopped dead in her tracks.

"Kendall! It's always, Kendall. I'm the one that

loves you, Beck."

Beck not realizing how dangerous Sally could be made no attempt to placate the crazed woman.

"In high school I turned you down, Sally" he snapped. "In college, I told you no. After Kendall left me and you offered, I said no...again."

The smoke in the room thickened. Her eyes stung as she struggled to keep sight of her grandmother. Heat and ash clung to every breath, making it difficult to inhale.

"But, you stopped him from hurting—,"

"Sally, we were teenagers. No one knew that your father abused you."

Kendall hadn't known about Beck and Sally's history. She could empathize with the need for a savior. She'd done the same with her decision to marry Beck.

"Darlin' we need to get out of this furnace."

Just like when Kendall pointed the gun at him, Cutler remained calm, ready for action. He must have been one heck of a Marine. The man was unflappable in a crisis.

"But you did and things got better for me after that," Sally cried and coughed in earnest.

"I didn't know anything. I just happened to be

walking by your house when I heard you screaming. All your silly little stunts have to stop. You're a nut case."

No. No, Beck.

Sally raised the gun. "Maybe you were right, Beck. You don't know anything, including who's best for you."

Sally pulled the trigger. When the bullet entered Beck's upper torso, he stumbled back a step, and then crumpled to the ground.

"You shot me," he cried out. Blood oozed between the fingers he pressed over the wound to staunch the flow.

"Shut up, Beck." Sally screamed, as she dropped to her knees beside him "You need to shut up before I put both of us out of our misery."

Abruptly, Kendall looked down to see Sally aim the gun at her.

"These men take and take. They never give."

All at once Kendall felt sorry for Sally. How much had she endured at the hands of a father that was supposed to love her?

Cutler had used the time during Beck and Sally's floor drama to stealthily scoop up her grandmother.

"Let's go, Red."

"I can't."

He gripped her arm. "This is not the time to play lone ranger."

She shook her head no. "I think Mrs. Elliott is in the bedroom. You go and I'll look for her."

He hesitated a second, then released her. "Make it fast, Kendall. I'll get your granny out and come back for you."

While Beck tussled with an attentive Sally, Kendall reached the bedroom. The shared wall with the bathroom was charred. Smoke was everywhere. Mrs. Elliott lay on the mattress, unmoving. Kendall hauled the woman up by the arms and folded her over her shoulders. She spied the melted plastic tubing sticking to a green portable oxygen cylinder on her way out the door.

She moved by memory to the exit. "Beck," she called, "Get out...explosion," she choked out the words. Kendall imagined her father moving through the youth center saving whom he could as he got her mother to safety. Was he as scared as she was now?

Sizzling air greeted her in the hallway. In her lungs, the sensation was worse than swallowing scalding hot coffee. The effort to descend the stairs with the added weight zapped her energy. With her turnout gear on, circumnavigating through a blaze this intense would be scary, without it...she was terrified. Without the flame-retardant suit, she could feel her body succumbing to the heat and smoke.

All of a sudden an explosion rocked the building. The foundation beneath her feet rolled. Kendall lost her grip, and both she and Mrs. Elliott went crashing down the stairs. The pain as she landed at an odd angle on her leg was excruciating. She tried to stand, but failed. The smoke was so thick she couldn't breathe, couldn't see. Thank God, Cutler had gotten Grandma Dinah to safety. She saw her mother's face, and then she saw Cutler's. Now, she understood why her father had run back into a burning building. Kendall prayed for her mother's forgiveness in that moment. The anger she'd felt and the unfound blame she laid on her parent fell away as she lay helpless on the ground. Did she and Cutler have the kind of love that risked everything...because she wasn't going to make it out.

With the last of her breath, she began to scream. "Stairs, help us."

With her tongue swollen and immobile in her dry mouth, Kendall collapsed onto her belly, her skin ablaze with heat. She felt her body afloat and the life drained from her limbs.

"I've got you, darlin'," she heard Cutler say in her haze.

She had to tell him how she felt before she left him. Why had she waited so long? She imagined her parents had uttered a message of love to each other before they were gone.

"Love...you, cowboy."

His wicked chuckle, deep and rich filled her head. "Love you, too, Lil' Red."

Epilogue

"Cutler, it's pouring outside," Kendall called from the futon, her favorite piece of furniture in the house.

"Perfect. The basket is packed and we're going to our special place. Then we're off to meet Dinah and Mrs. Elliott."

Every time it rained in the past month since the fire, Cutler loaded them up in the truck and drove to the airport—back to their beginning. He never got enough of making out with her in the rain, getting drenched from head to toe.

"I'm glad they decided to be roommates," Kendall laughed. "Will Nathan, Trace, and the rest of the gang be joining us?"

"I'm glad you decided to accept Captain Brady's job offer, Red. It's not every day we have a firefighter that stays behind in a burning building, wearing no gear to save an incapacitated victim." Cutler came up behind her, circling her waist in his strong arms, before cupping her full breasts in his palms. "You make a decision on my offer, yet?"

Cutler's marriage proposal came while she lay strapped in the back of an EMT transport with an oxygen mask over her face.

"Um," Kendall crooned when he kissed her cheek. Thirty days vacation had kept her in Key West after her assignment ended. After she called for Beck to exit the burning building, he had gotten himself and Sally outside. With a lot of encouragement from Trace and Lance, her ex had returned to Cockrell. Sally would stand trial for arson and aggravated assault for starters, if and when the courts deemed her competent. "Yep, I've thought about your proposition. I'll tell you once we reach my grandmother's house."

In her ear, he whispered, "You gonna keep your man in suspense?"

She laughed. "Shouldn't our friends be there when I announce the date?"

Cutler spun her around. His large hands circled her waist and she felt giddy when her feet left the ground as he twirled them around.

"Sounds like we'll be planning another wedding," he hollered. "Tell your granny to expect the Hobo Alley contingent for dinner. Nathan and Symphony, Rachel and Claudia, and Adam will appreciate your granny's cooking."

Her feet touched the ground, but her heart soared high above the clouds, filled with love and hope for their future.

"What about Trace?" she asked.

"He's at the hospital visiting his sleeping beauty."

Kendall said a silent prayer for the unconscious woman Trace had saved during the fire.

"Has anyone responded to the Jane Doe alert?"

"Not yet. Considering she wore a wig and had no identification, I think she might be on the run."

"If there's anyone that can slay her dragons and bring her back to the land of the living, it's Trace." She stepped closer in his arms. "You ok with loading the truck without me? I need to grab the jerseys I had designed for the kids at the youth center."

"The kids will love them."

She looked into the bluest eyes of the man she adored. "I love you, Cutler Stevens."

"I love you too, Lil' Red."

Kendall kissed him. Her heart, the lovesick organ, and life were an open book to Cutler. There was nothing left to conceal. He knew all her secrets and…he still wanted forever with her by his side.

If you loved Cutler and Kendall's story, read
Nathan and Symphony's story
In
CHASING FLAMES.

Look for
Trace and Victoria's story
In
COMMANDING HEAT.

About the Author

Siera London knew she wanted to be a writer when she kept searching for interesting topics to write about. She tried non-fiction writing first, but when the words on the page bored her to tears, she decided to write what she enjoyed reading. By day, she is a nurse practitioner at a private pediatric clinic. At night, she writes sizzling romances with emotion and humor.

A lover of all things culinary, Siera lives in South Florida with her husband, and a color-patch tabby named Frie. When she's not writing, she's reading, teaching, or volunteering. She's a member of Romance Writers of America.

Connect with Siera London

Visit my website: www.sieralondon.com
Follow me on Facebook:
https://www.facebook.com/authorsieralondon
E-mail me at: sieralondonwrites@gmail.com

Dear Reader,

Check out the rest of the books in the Dallas Fire & Rescue Kindle World here!

http://paigetylertheauthor.com/BooksDallasFire AndRescueKind...

If you loved CONCEALING FIRE, then check out my Bachelors of Shell Cove series.

Visit www.sieralondon.com for more stories by Siera London!

Want to know more about me or join the conversation about my books?

1. Sign-up for my newsletter at www.sieralondon.com. You will get updates on any new novels, book signings, and giveaways.

2. Follow my Amazon Author page at http://amzn.to/1Oce1Ht.

3. Write a review on Amazon and invite me to your reading group. Please consider leaving a review. Book reviews to an author are the equivalent of engine oil for a car—in other words, they are vital.

4. Go to my Facebook page and "like" me. My Facebook family is welcoming and I host a mean Facebook party. Here's the link:

https://www.facebook.com/authorsieralondon.

I truly appreciate your support, and someday I hope to tell you in person the impact you've had on my life. Wishing you all the best that life has to offer.

Hugs,
Siera

Made in the USA
Charleston, SC
23 January 2017